ANGEL ROARS

SOUL FORGE BOOK FIVE

LESLIE CLAIRE WALKER

sfp

My name is Night Sanchez. Every choice I make leads me toward redemption.

Although I prevented the Archangel Gabriel from turning an innocent normal into an obedient magical soldier, I know he'll be back. I watch for him. I wait.

But another enemy returns: The Source of Evil.

This time he's not after me. His target? Humans. All of them.

The Angel and I have never been more powerful—or more vulnerable. How do you stop a foe that hides in plain sight? An enemy who can be everywhere at once? An enemy that can't be killed?

I don't just want to save as many people as possible. I want to save them all.

I can't do it alone. My found family rallies at my side. Together, we'll roll the dice. We'll lay it on all the line.

Nothing—and no one—will ever be the same.

ALSO BY LESLIE CLAIRE WALKER

THE AWAKENED MAGIC SAGA

THE SOUL FORGE

(The Complete Series)

Angel Hunts

Angel Rises

Angel Falls

Angel Strikes

Angel Roars

Angel Burns

THE FAERY CHRONICLES

(The Complete Series)

Faery Novice

Faery Prophet

Faery Sovereign

SHORT STORY COLLECTIONS

Ink & Blood

Ink & Stars

Ink & Sword

For Chester

CHAPTER 1

R ARE SUNLIGHT STREAMED from the clear blue sky, a benediction for my sleepy neighborhood. The ice coating the bare branches of the maples along the street glittered like diamonds. I inhaled January frost, my exhale fogging the air. The tips of my fingers felt chilled inside my black leather gloves. I hadn't gotten used to the pack on my back or what it camouflaged. The melting slick on the sidewalk made temporary peace with the soles of my boots.

Peace. What a strange word. An uncommon feeling.

Beside me, Faith slipped, catching her feet a split second before she tumbled into the snow piled at the curb. Her cheeks flushed with the cold as she held out her arms to help with balance. Her long black hair gleamed in the morning light, her brown eyes filled with humor. Bundled up in her black down coat and wool scarf, matching wool mittens on her hands, she reminded me of her younger self. She'd been a child once. Not anymore.

The halo that enveloped her body—an expression of her life force and magic—shone equal parts silver and gold. The silver had been hers since she'd been born. The gold belonged to the god she carried inside, the Awakened.

It had only been a month or so since the Awakened had come alive within her. Since she'd gone from being only my daughter to becoming the vessel for the god of magic itself. She'd spent most of that time in Texas, creating a safe space for other magical children. Having her here in Portland, even for a couple of days, meant everything.

We'd left Red at home in his pajamas, building a fire in the hearth, promising to bring back breakfast and coffee from the winter wonderland. The kiss he'd given me before I'd stepped out the door and locked down its magical protections glowed with so much warmth and promise, I hadn't wanted to leave home.

Home—another strange word.

He had his own place, and I had mine, but we'd spent most of our time of late at a friend's house, fortified against the forces of evil, fighting to stave off the oncoming Apocalypse. No one had time for snowy mornings and leisurely breakfasts and family. We'd all been too busy making hard choices. Surviving.

"You're thinking about it again," Faith said. "You should stop."

"The rest of the worlds aren't going away. We have enemies. We have to stay alert."

She sighed. "It's your training. If you were a normal, you'd be talking about the glorious sunshine."

"If I were a normal," I said, "a lot of things would be different."

I hadn't been a regular, non-magical girl, though. Not since I was a toddler. My ability to meld my consciousness with other minds had come on hard and fast, disturbing my parents' sense of good and evil and taking us all down a dark, narrow road to Hell.

In the end, they'd been killed. The Order of the Blood Moon—an order of magical assassins—had become my family. They'd taught me strategy and obedience. They'd taught me to use my magic to kill, and all the blood on my hands had shattered my soul.

I'd left them behind years ago, going on the run with Faith. By the grace of the powers and the spirits of the dead, my soul had been created anew. Still, my Order training hadn't left me. If anything, I relied on it more every day.

We rounded the corner, moving from the quiet of the neighborhood onto Hawthorne. The street wasn't as busy as it should be because of the snow and ice. There were more pedestrians than cars. Lots of families out and about. The parents looked relaxed, released from their workaday routines. The kids looked overjoyed.

A block or so ahead, in the shadow of newly built apartments, the coffee shop's sign shone brightly.

"We've been left alone for less than a week," I said. "No Order assassins. No magical attacks. No archangels on the doorstep. That won't last long. It's hard to let it go."

"Thirty minutes," she said. "Can you do half an hour?"

I looked at her. "Why?"

She slowed to a stop. "Because I miss you, Night. I have a job to do, and I'm going to have to go back to it. The time will fly and this will all be over. I want to spend some time with my mom. You know, like most people. Regular people."

I adjusted the straps of my pack. Most people carried stuff in their backpacks. Most people didn't have a full set of black-feathered angel wings folded down to a compact twelve inches, hidden underneath waxed canvas and Italian leather. Most people didn't serve as the human host of the Angel of Death.

La Muerte—the Angel—laughed. The sound echoed inside my head and rumbled inside my chest.

Once upon a time, he'd been my prisoner, then my passenger. Now, I didn't know exactly what to call him. We were becoming one, he and I. I feared how that would turn out for me. For the people I loved.

I had a lot to worry about. Faith was asking me not to spend my thoughts and energy on any of it for thirty lousy minutes. I could do that. Couldn't I?

I took a deep breath and blew it out in a stream of fog and mist. "Okay."

We walked into the coffee shop, which had its heat cranked up to a level that reminded me frogs could be convinced to boil to death. The tables to our right had been taken by computer people, the sofas and comfy chairs to our left peppered with readers and conversationalists.

Nate, the brown-eyed kid with the lady-killer smile behind the counter in front took orders, an army of three behind him to execute.

The sounds system played a series of Linkin Park tunes. The line was short, and the people unremarkable. Everyone in their proper place, eyes on their own business or staring off into space, daydreaming. The short hall that led to the restrooms and back exit was clear.

We'd arrived just in time—a group pushed through the door behind us, filling up the line, pulling off hats and gloves, murmuring amongst themselves.

A normal coffee shop. A place for regular people with their shiny non-magical halos.

After a couple of false starts, Faith asked for three bacon-and-egg sandwiches and three coconut-milk lattes. She wandered off to the side to wait while I fished crumpled cash from my front pocket.

Nate pitched his tenor low, for my ears only. "You see that guy in the corner?"

I raised a brow, taking my eyes off my palm full of money to meet his gaze. "What?"

"Something's wrong with him."

I glanced over my shoulder, zeroing in on a bearded guy in a green knit cap and matching coat. He leaned against the back wall, go-cup of coffee in hand, lost in his thoughts. His white skin looked pale, the lenses of his silver wire–framed glasses casting shadows beneath his eyes. The corners of his mouth turned down, trembling. He shifted his weight from one hiking-booted foot to another. His halo had no shine —no, he had no halo.

No, that wasn't right.

His halo had been overtaken. Overwhelmed by nothing at all.

Nate's voice interrupted my thoughts. "I don't know why I'm telling you this, except that you look like you can handle yourself. Like you'd know what to do with that guy."

I looked at him. He pressed his lips together and kept his jaw square, as if he were trying to keep it together, but his eyes held a wildness that reflected the truth—that he was freaked out.

I handed him a twenty. He made change as if there was nothing wrong.

"Keep it," I said.

He shoved three dollar bills into the tip jar. "What do I do?"

"Give the breakfast order to Faith when it comes up. I'll check out your trouble."

His relief was so immediate and thick, I could've cut it with a knife. "Thank you."

"Don't thank me yet," I said.

I tried to catch Faith's eye, but she'd glanced down at her phone, thumbs racing across the surface. Judging by the softness of her expression, she was texting her girlfriend, Corey. She wouldn't look up without my touch or my raised voice, and I didn't want to draw attention.

I started toward the trouble, my magic rising with me to fill every cell, every molecule, until it pushed up against the edges of my skin. I held it in check, ready to strike, ready to slip into his mind and bind him to the spot where he stood if necessary.

He blinked, climbing out of his imagination and into the present. He raised his chin, meeting my gaze with unexpected boldness for a stranger.

There was nothing in his eyes. Not a single emotion. Not a coherent thought. He looked empty, but he smiled at me. The gesture made my skin crawl.

I sensed no magic in him. No power that he could unleash in this place. But every inch of his nothing-halo screamed that he was a threat. That he, and he alone, could hurt me. Hurt Faith. Harm all of us.

I picked up my pace, making a beeline for him. Placing myself between him and as many people as I could shelter with my body and my power.

He turned on his heel, dropping his go-cup, which exploded in an espresso-and-foamed-milk bomb on the floor. The people closest to him leapt out of the way in a cascade of *whoas* and laughter and scrape of chair legs on concrete. He shoved his way through the people in line and out the door.

I threaded my way through the crowd to follow, stepping out into a gust of icy wind, my feet unsteady on the slick sidewalk. I looked left, then right, catching sight of my target standing in front of the bright blue taqueria next door.

I sent my magic barreling for him, sliding into his consciousness and pinning him to the spot where he stood.

The sight of his own reflection in the taqueria window captured him. He marked the hat and coat, the fact that his glasses felt crooked, and the way his skin looked bleached, as if all the blood had drained from his face and hands.

His name was Mark.

His last memory was of stepping out his front door this morning, keys to his truck jingling in hand, and heading up the salted slope of the sidewalk to the apartment parking lot. A crow cawed from its perch in the ice-laden, bony branches of the oak behind the building. The wind kicked up, blowing from the Columbia River Gorge in the east, whipping the branches into a clacking, crackling frenzy. The wind seemed to find every seam and space in his coat, chilling him to the marrow.

His girlfriend had been out of town for a week, and he was headed to the airport to pick her up. He couldn't wait to taste her sweet mouth and run his hands through her long brown hair. A week was too long.

Then he'd spied the woman from 7B, a nurse heading home from her overnight shift. She liked to wear pink scrubs. They looked good on her.

He'd moved aside on the walk to give her the right of way—it was only polite, and he'd been raised to care about that. She'd laid a hand on his arm as he smiled in greeting, which was weird. Usually she kept her hands in her pockets.

His vision grayed out. For a second, he thought he might pass out. Maybe he was having a heart attack. Maybe a seizure.

Didn't make sense.

Then his vision blacked out. There was nothing else. Nothing until he'd somehow come to, standing in front of the taqueria window, staring at his reflection.

He knew where he was. He ate at this place a couple of times a month. He loved the pollo verde. He loved the chips and salsa. He especially loved the horchata. But he'd been on his way to the airport, not on his way to breakfast tacos. He plucked his phone from the back pocket of his jeans. No, he only thought about it. His arms and hands refused to obey, as if he'd frozen to the spot. As if someone else had taken control of him.

That was a crazy thought. This was the real world, and that shit didn't happen here.

Fear bloomed in his heart like a poisonous flower as I came to stand in front of him, blocking his view of the window.

His halo had shifted in the time it'd taken me to walk to him. Where before there had been nothing, now the normal shine reasserted itself—health and vitality returning. A sense of self. A sense of consciousness.

I met his gaze, searching him for any signs of magic. There were none.

He wanted to ask me who I was. What I'd done to him and why.

I let go of him, noting the fine motor movements as his own systems of balance and being took over again. He blinked at me.

"Are you Night?" he asked.

My turn to show surprise. "Have we met?"

"No," he said. "At least I don't think so. But I know your name. And I know that you're Death."

He said it just like that—with a capital D.

"What happened to me?" he asked.

"I don't know," I said, although it wasn't one-hundred-percent true.

He acted as if he'd been possessed, but I couldn't tell him that.

He swallowed hard. "Can I go now?"

I had no reason to hold him—at least, none that I could see right now. He was already freaked out. Judging from the tremor in his fingers, not too far from being on his way to panic—or rage.

I opened my mouth to invite him to sit down. I'd buy him a new cup of coffee and we could sort things out with more time and space, although I had no faith that more of either would give us better answers.

The words died on my tongue.

As I glanced past him, I caught sight of a familiar figure across the street, bundled in a black leather jacket and leaning against the side of an empty, darkened bar. He bore all of his weight on one black-booted foot, the other braced against the wall. He'd hooked his thumbs in the front pockets of his black jeans. The once-white script emblazoned on his black T-shirt read, *Ride the Lightning*. He had black hair, short and thick.

For a heartbeat, his hair appeared to be made of fire, writhing flames of orange, yellow, red, and blue. He had three eyes, two in the usual places and a third in the center of his forehead. He wore glittering, diamond-like armor, a sword with a golden hilt sheathed on his back.

Then his normal-guy façade returned. He could've been anyone—except for the way the air bent around his body in response to the immense power he carried.

"Go on," I said absently to Mark.

He didn't need to be told twice. He walked away as fast as his feet would take him, leaving me standing on one side of Hawthorne and the archangel Michael on the other.

CHAPTER 2

I LOOKED BOTH ways, raising a hand in thanks to the driver behind the wheel of the silver minivan who stopped with a squeal of brakes and sliding tires to let me cross the street. I scanned the parking lot of the liquor store on Michael's right and the strip of shops to his left. There was no magical or mundane threat, and few places for one to hide.

A woman walking her golden retriever was the only incoming traffic. She passed Michael with a shiver, but her dog paused, giving the archangel a sniff. Michael hunkered down to the retriever's level, cupping its face in his palms, pressing his forehead to the dog's.

It was sweet. And that was a word I'd never use to describe Michael. Not in a million years.

As I planted a foot on the curb, he stood up, knees popping, sending the dog on its way. Michael's voice sounded too big for his body—too big for the entire world. "Night."

The last time I'd seen him, he'd given me an ultimatum. He'd wanted me to hand over a woman's soul so that he could use it to strike a blow against our ultimate enemy. Not only had I said no, I'd set fire to his plans.

"You here to kill me?" I asked. "It's a little public, don't you think?"

He laughed. "If I wanted you dead—"

I interrupted. "I'd already be toast."

"I came to talk," he said.

"Lecture or warning?"

"I don't get another choice?"

I shrugged. "Asking from experience."

"Why are we at odds, Night?"

"Because I won't do what you ask me to unless I think it's right," I said. "And that pisses you off."

"That's fair," he said.

There was no such thing as fair. Not for any of us.

Exhibit 1: The woman whose soul I'd refused to give up—Luna was her name—had only wanted a normal life. The archangel Gabriel had torpedoed that wish by gifting her with magic her body and soul had no hope in hell of handling. To get back to good, she had to tame a Horseman of the Apocalypse and find a way to share her body and soul with it.

I'd bet for her, Michael against.

That she'd managed to stand up and handle business gave the rest of us a chance to turn the tide at the end of the world.

"You understand why I did what I did?" I asked.

He nodded.

"So what's up?" I asked. "What merits an in-person visit?"

"The End is back."

He didn't mean the end of the world. He meant the architect of the Apocalypse. Not the monotheistic Satan, supposedly the opposite of God, but a being who was literally the opposite of creation. Not destruction, but the void where no oxygen—no creation, no life, no love—could live. The End, capital E.

I'd met him not long ago, when my family and I had invaded the Order location where I'd been made into a killer. We'd gone in to rescue magical children who were being murdered, their power and souls fed to the End. We'd been too late to save most of them, but we'd found a handful still alive.

If *La Muerte* embodied the ice cold of the grave, the End carried the cold of the void. Where the Angel represented the force of natural death—natural law, the cycle of life—the End stood for the opposite—no law, no natural world. The End meant nothingness.

The Apocalypse wasn't some mythical battle of good versus evil. It was a fight pitting the forces of true life against those of true death.

The Angel and I defeated the End during our battle at the Order, but we hadn't destroyed him. I didn't know whether he could be destroyed. Like the other Elder powers I'd met, present company included, chances were he could not be killed.

"I hoped we would have more time," I said.

Michael raised his chin, looking beyond me.

I turned to follow his gaze.

Faith stood in front of the taqueria, carrying a drinks tray with a paper bag full of breakfast balanced on top. Her mouth hung open. She'd never seen Michael, but she understood who I was talking with. If her human self didn't recognize him, the god inside her did.

I held up a hand to signal her, my meaning clear.

Stay where you are.

"How long is she here in Portland?" Michael asked.

"Why?"

"She's an asset. We may need her."

She was powerful, but she was also my kid. I wanted to protect her, but *want to* and *able to* weren't the same.

"Where is the End?" I asked.

"Everywhere," Michael said.

I raised a brow.

Michael mirrored the gesture. "The man you confronted on the street?"

"He was a normal. Something happened to him. He didn't remember what."

"Like someone possessed," Michael said.

In a flash, I connected the goddamn dots. "When I first laid eyes on him in the coffee shop, he had no halo. No, that's not right—he had one. It took up space, and I could see it, but it was made of nothing."

"Who else bears that signature?"

The End.

"How is that possible? That man—Mark—he had no magic. What's his vulnerability?"

"The End doesn't require either."

"That's not how this works."

Michael sighed, brushing off my words. "You believe the End is one being. He is not. He is the consciousness of the void. He is its malevolence. He can appear as one being, embodied for a purpose. But his natural state is fragmented, scattered. He's taking advantage of that to push the worlds closer to Apocalypse."

We'd been fighting to keep that from happening from the moment the Angel of Death had arrived on the scene. We'd won small victories. Sometimes, they felt like more than that, as if they meant something.

But there were now three Horsemen walking the worlds. Famine, who was the first of us to possess a human and act in the human world, and who sided with the End. Luna, possessed by Pestilence, who had negotiated a way to hold on to her humanity, and who sheltered in Faery while she and Pestilence learned how to live with each other. Lastly, there was me, a former Order assassin, who carried the Angel of Death. The fourth Horseman had yet to join us, but it would happen—sooner rather than later.

That, I understood. That, I could work with or around. If Luna and I could remain who we were at our core even while possessed by a Horseman, then perhaps we could make sure the fourth Horseman's human vessel had the same chance. Worst case, it would be two Horseman on the side of destruction and two on the side of life. Equal odds.

But I didn't get what Michael was talking about. I'd never heard of any being who could break into that many parts without dying.

"His natural state?"

"Yes," he said. "You've heard stories about how the Devil can possess any man—or many men at once?"

"The Devil made me do it. I've never believed that. It lets humans off the hook too easily. You don't have to take responsibility for your actions if you can say the bogeyman forced you."

"What if it's true? Not the way you've heard or understood it, but what if it's true of the End?"

"Then we're screwed," I said. "With seven billion potential enemies."

"Or a few dozen."

"That's still too many moving parts for me to track," I said. "You're gonna have to spell it out for me. What are these few dozen people up to?"

"They're signs," he said.

Just the one word, but it was enough. "Signs of the Apocalypse?"

Michael nodded.

I tried to wrap my head around that. "A few dozen people possessed by the End, setting off magical, apocalyptic bombs?"

"No, Night. Hear me: the people themselves are the signs."

"That makes zero sense."

"Only if you think of signs as water turning to blood or eclipses," he said.

Of course that was how I thought of them. Spectacles. Unmistakable, earth-shattering events. But if they were smaller? Harder to notice?

"I don't suppose you're planning to tell me what they are, then? Because I know there's not a book I can read for clues."

"Unfortunately not," he said.

"Because the Bible isn't accurate."

"It holds some truth, Night."

"But not all."

"No. Not all." He sighed. "There are many possible signs. I can only tell you that the first one has already come to pass, and that the last one will involve you."

"Me?"

He showed me a wry half-grin, his eyes shaded with commiseration.

That much care about what I thought—about what I had to face if what he said was true—surprised me. He'd made a habit of only showing up when he needed something from me, not when I needed him.

"Why me?" I asked.

"I wish I knew."

"You're the right hand of a god, and you don't know?"

"I wield the fiery sword of protection," he said. "It pains me not to know."

I felt sure that archangels could lie with the best of them, but I didn't sense untruth from Michael. He really did seem sorry, but that didn't change the facts he'd relayed.

"Can you tell me more about the other signs?" I asked.

"I can't," he said.

"Something else you don't know?"

He nodded.

"Can the signs be stopped?"

"No."

A word without room for doubt or maneuvering.

"It's not possible to stop the chain reaction once the signs have begun to manifest," he said. "But if anyone can find a way to do the impossible, it will be you."

I wanted to hate him right here and now. I had plenty of experience doing just that. But I couldn't seem to find it in me now that we had the next fight on our hands. "You're allowed to help me?"

He shook his head. "I'm not supposed to be here at all."

But he was. "So breaking the rules isn't just for me and mine, then."

"Don't count on my help, Night."

"I never do," I said.

"This will get bad. Worse than it's ever been. Do you understand?"

Worse? I could barely imagine such a thing, but all my life things had gone from bad to worse, and I understood that there was no such thing as rock bottom, not really. Only the depth of pain and misery we were willing to tolerate or could survive.

"Do you intend to work against me?" I asked.

He didn't respond.

I took a step forward. I wanted to get close—to demand an answer. I wanted a promise from him that he wouldn't try to stop me from doing what I knew to be right. If we were going to work together, openly or in secret, we would have to trust each other. He hadn't yet proven that I could count on him. He needed to put up or shut up.

As I crossed the edge of his magic—the place where the air bent around him—the power emanating from his skin felt like hurricane-force wind. It stopped me in my tracks, picking up the magic I shot at him and shredding it as if it were made of confetti.

It knocked me off balance. It made my world spin.

I closed my eyes for a heartbeat, bracing my feet on the concrete, taking shallow breaths to calm the sudden flip of my stomach and the nausea that stormed through me.

When I looked for Michael again, he was gone.

CHAPTER 3

THE FIRE IN the hearth looked dangerous instead of inviting, as if any second the flames that lapped at the wrought iron screen meant to escape and set the whole place alight. Coltrane streamed from the TV in the corner, the volume low enough that the notes whispered along my nerves, igniting every one.

Dust motes floated in the air behind Red's wet, shaggy salt-and-pepper hair. He'd thrown on a pair of faded jeans and a black hoodie, the toes of his bare feet digging into the pile of the rug. His grass-and-earth halo looked like an easy morning at home, grounded and comfortable. His lips curved, but his smile faded as Faith made her way to the table and I began the process of kicking off boots and shrugging off the backpack that camouflaged my wings.

He read the gist of what happened in both of us, his magic taking stock of our hearts. Faith's fear. My fear and anger.

"Michael," I said.

He thinned his lips beneath his mustache. His subtle East Texas drawl grew more pronounced with each word. "Michael showed up on the street. On a street full of normals."

Faith set the coffee tray and breakfast bag down on the black-painted dining table on the far wall. She unzipped her coat, shrugging out of it and rearranging the hem of her dark plum sweater, which in a fit of static electricity had climbed halfway up her midriff and stuck to the black T-shirt she wore underneath. "Night says he wasn't an asshole."

My favorite name for Michael. Most of the time it fit. "I did not say that. The End is back. There are signs of the Apocalypse."

Red folded his arms across his chest.

"Sorry to be the bearer of bad news," Faith said.

"Is there any other kind?" he asked.

Faith opened her mouth to retort, then snapped it shut. She yanked off her coat and marched around the corner to her room.

"When are Sunday and Miguel arriving?" he asked.

"Soon as they can manage," I said, dropping my house keys in the dish on the entry table.

He met my gaze. "We're not gonna get that break we hoped for, are we?"

"Not the way we wanted it," I said.

Newly engaged people should have some time to celebrate. Most people took a moment to revel in the thought of spending the rest of their lives together and lose themselves in each other's arms, at least for a while.

We were not most people.

Red stepped up to help me out of the backpack, and then my coat, which we'd modified to make room for my wings. His touch was a comfort and an enticement. For a split second, I wanted to run away from the avalanche of bullshit roaring our way.

The moment passed.

I didn't run away from trouble. I ran toward it. It was in my DNA.

My wings unfurled to their full length. Relief surged through the muscles of my shoulders and back. I stretched my left arm forward and across my chest, then my right.

He slipped his arms around my waist. "What did I say before you and Faith left the house?"

"*Be careful* doesn't mean *take no risks*."

"No, it doesn't. Not where you're concerned."

"The world's on fire," I said.

"Not yet." He planted a kiss on the back of my neck that sent a shiver along my skin.

A knock sounded on the door. The protections had sent no warning, nor did I hear the thud of an electric-shocked enemy hitting the concrete.

Red sighed and slid out of the way as I turned the knob.

Sunday Sloan stood at the threshold, looking like a former Order assassin—or a house burglar. Black knit hat on her blond curls, black coat and pants, black winter boots with proper traction. I caught the outline of a knife in her pants pocket. Her pale cheeks were flushed, the blue of her eyes darker than usual. Her halo shone with rose-gold fire, her magic ready to fly.

Even if she didn't live that far away, with icy streets in Portland, she had to have flown to get here so quickly. And flying wasn't her magical superpower. Blinding her enemies was.

She answered the question on my face, her voice like water flowing over rocks. "I got here so fast because I put chains on my tires."

"On your Prius?"

She shook her head. "No more Prius. Subaru."

"Where'd you get this one?"

"Stole it," she said dryly.

Red laughed. "You always prepared?"

She winked at him. "For anything, Jennings."

Their friendship had grown solid over the last months—an unexpected blessing. My best friend and former lover and the man I'd just agreed to marry liked and trusted each other.

I turned toward the table, cocking my head as an invitation to follow. The food and drink on the table was cool at this point, but that was nothing a little microwave time couldn't cure.

"Something in there for me?" Sunday asked.

"I'll split my sandwich with you while we talk about signs of the Apocalypse," Red said.

She clapped him on the back and slipped out of her coat, hanging it on the back of a dining chair. "The only clue we have is that guy, Mark, and you let him get away, Sanchez."

I popped Red's—and Sunday's—breakfast in the microwave to heat. "Mark ran from me—I don't blame him. By the time I understood he was more than he seemed, he was long gone."

"Do you think Michael intentionally distracted you?" she asked.

"I wouldn't put it past him."

"But?"

"He seemed to be skirting the rules, trying to help. I didn't feel any deceit."

"That leaves us with what? An indeterminate number of temporarily possessed people out there, and no clue how to find them? We can't search the city, hoping to lay eyes on one of them."

"No," I said. "But we can use our resources."

"The Watchers?" she asked.

"Yes, the Watchers."

The magical law, among whom we had friends.

Red pulled his phone from his back pocket and dialed. Addie answered fast, as if she expected the call. He slipped through the door of our bedroom, his voice low and steady as he filled her in.

"She just got her house back," Sunday said.

"Should've known it wouldn't last."

It was Addie's job to track magical beings who entered the Portland city limits. The ones who minded their own business and posed no danger to others, she left alone. She got rid of those who posed too great a risk.

"We should head to her place as soon as Miguel gets here," I said.

Red returned, phone in hand. "She was already up and cooking."

She had a way of knowing when someone was coming over. She knew how to open a path to their heart and their history right away—through their stomach. She prepared what her target loved to eat. Whatever would draw out the most information verbally and magically.

The front door opened. Miguel entered in a flurry of ice crystals, which he shook off his black coat and hat like a wet dog, splattering the entry table and floor. His black hair had finally begun to grow after the enemy had chopped it off at the nape of his neck. Now, it almost brushed his shoulders. Wariness filled his brown eyes. His purple bruise of a halo roiled, like waves crashing against a shore.

He was a chameleon—he could shift his physical body to copy anyone he spent enough time with. If the person possessed magic, he could copy that, too. It was never one-hundred-percent foolproof. There would always be some memory or bit of information the chameleon's power couldn't get deep enough to master, but it was almost always enough to make a chameleon one-hundred-percent lethal.

Like Sunday, Miguel had been an Order operative. The Order had sent him to kill us, but instead he'd come over to our side.

"I was starting to get comfortable," he said. "Two, three days of comfort. Believe it or not, I actually liked it. Know what it reminds me of, that feeling? Before the Order."

Before they'd taken him and turned him into what he was now.

I happened to know he had a shit childhood. "Nostalgia is a liar."

"Desire isn't," he said.

The soul wanted what it wanted, end of story. I got it.

He started to take off his coat.

I raised a hand to stop him.

"We're moving out already?"

"We are."

"I haven't even introduced my surprise yet."

We weren't expecting anyone else. "I hate surprises."

"We might need this one," he said. "Firepower. Backup. She's got it all."

Behind him, someone stepped into the apartment. I glanced past him to see a head full of brown hair knotted into eight snake-like braids and an orange halo filled with writhing strands of black. I knew that hair, and that halo.

They belonged to Beth, apprentice to the serpent from the Garden of Eden. She'd fought beside us twice in the last month. She had a habit of saying uncomfortable things that I didn't want to hear, but she'd never failed to come through.

"I found her on the sidewalk out front," he said. "Pacing and mumbling to herself, like she was trying to talk herself into coming up. Weird, I'll admit. But she's a gift horse. Or a Trojan horse."

"Hey—standing right here," she said, elbowing Miguel out of her path. "I know, you didn't have time to miss me."

Beth wore a burnt-orange sweater at least two sizes too big for her small frame, black jeans, and purple rain boots. Her purple wool pea coat would've been perfect for a Houston winter day, but that couldn't have been more wrong for rainy Portland. She'd slung an orange backpack onto her right shoulder, the kind of bag you take on a day trip.

I met her gaze. "What are you doing here?"

Her black glasses framed green eyes that missed nothing. Including my ambivalence about her sudden, convenient presence.

"Malek sent me. He said something had happened this morning and he needed me on the ground here—again. Honestly, I'm kinda pissed. I didn't sign up to be his eyes and ears on the ground two thousand miles away from home."

She hadn't "signed up" at all.

Malek—the serpent from the Garden of Eden, cursed into human form—had made Beth his apprentice to save her life. In the process, she'd given up her mortality and begun to learn the art of magical tattooing, which had been Malek's chosen profession for I didn't know how long. She popped off about things that weren't her business and stuck her nose in the dark corners of the world. Curiosity killed the cat.

It had killed Beth, too, at least once. Her boss had resurrected her.

"What did he say?" I asked.

"That Michael put in a live appearance. And that an enemy had returned—the Big Bad."

These things had happened inside of the hour. I'd called only Sunday and Miguel. Only our crew knew the score, and none of them would've sent word to Malek.

"How does he know all that?" I asked.

"I can see what you're thinking," Beth said.

"No. You can't."

She had no mind- or heart- or soul-reading talent. She had sigils tattooed on her body that did various convenient things, poison for blood, and an affinity for trouble.

"Okay," she said. "Let me tell you what you should think, because I suck at lying and if you're going to be pissed off at me, I'd rather get it out of the way now. Does that work for you?"

I blinked at her.

"Malek bugged you," she said. "Well, not you specifically."

I stared at her.

"You're wondering whether he did it physically or magically, but he's never been to your place and neither have I and if we tried to do something as stupid as bugging you or your place, you'd have felt it, right? And don't even worry about your phone because you would know about that, too."

She was right. I would.

I put two and two together before she could throw another run-on sentence my way. "If he didn't bug me, that means another one of us. We all ward our spaces and ourselves. There's no way he could've gotten to us without our permission. A few days ago, you had permission, Beth."

"It wasn't my choice," she said. "He told me to do it, so I did, because that's what I do. It's what I'm supposed to do."

"What are y'all talking about?" Red asked.

"The tattoos," I said. "The break-the-glass-it's-an-emergency tattoos she inked a few days ago on everyone except you, me, and our time-traveling friend, Charlie."

We'd needed those tattoos. They'd saved lives after Pestilence had cursed most of us with a soul sickness. Beth's magical tattoos bought us time until we found a way to remove the curse.

Sunday and Miguel. Beth had tattooed them. On the walk back from Mark and Michael, I'd called both of them.

Sunday spoke through gritted teeth. "You spied on me."

Beth frowned. "I just told you—I didn't want to do it."

"But you did," I said. "What else are the tattoos designed for? What other information do they relay?"

"Magical interactions."

"That's all?"

"Vital signs?"

"Blood pressure? Oxygen levels? Reserves of magical power?"

Beth shook her head. "More like, *is your heart still beating.*"

Sunday glanced at me. "Are all the powerful men we know douches? Malek. Michael. Is there any end to it?"

I shrugged.

Sunday eyed Red. "What about you, Jennings?"

"I'm staying out of this," he said.

I understood why Malek wanted to keep tabs. He couldn't control the situation. He couldn't control me. He'd lived forever, from the beginning of time, but he had a secret vulnerability that he'd shared with me. I'd agreed to hold the information close.

Alone, I was no danger to him. But if all four Horseman walked the earth, we would be. All it would take was one more.

Malek and I were allies because he'd chosen to align himself with the side of life in this fight. He'd offered help in the form of Beth. But he wasn't a friend.

I'd begun to think of Beth as one. My mistake.

"Were you planning to tell us?" I asked.

"Yes," she said—not too quickly, and no stalling.

Her halo didn't shift or change. She didn't twitch or look away. I heard no lie.

She clasped her hands behind her neck. "I mean, what dumb story am I supposed to tell about why I'm here? Malek said to make something up. He has a reason; he just didn't share it with me. Sometimes he doesn't. Okay, a lot of times he doesn't. He wanted me to lie, but I'm not all right with that. I wasn't all right with it in the first place."

"You were willing to disobey his order," I said. "What's the price for that?"

"Blood," she said. "Pain."

"Even for you?"

"I don't know," she said. "I've never crossed him, and I'm only doing it now because I have to work with you—I *want* to work with you—and if we can't trust each other, how can we do that?"

"Great speech," I said. "You give it to Malek, too?"

"Yes, actually."

No lie there, either. But I had to wonder what else she'd hedged about or left out. I had to wonder whether she could be trusted at all. If I couldn't trust her—

"You want my life's story?" she asked. "I can give it to you, along with the names of witnesses who can vouch for all of my awesomeness and all of my character defects, but that will take time we don't have. Or we can work together and figure it out along the way."

Or I could send her back to Malek. I let that show on my face.

"Don't you dare send me back there," she said. "Not now. If you try, I'll cut you."

Sunday stared at her. "You should be begging our forgiveness."

Beth stared right back. "I don't do begging."

"Do you apologize?"

Beth let her hands fall to her sides. "Sorry. Sincerely."

I looked at Sunday. She shrugged. Violently.

"I'm asking to stay," Beth said. "Please."

I let Beth stew for a moment. One, she deserved it. Two, I'd just noticed something that started a flutter in the pit of my stomach. We'd been talking out here for a few minutes and the shit had hit the fan. Raised voices and angry words. But Faith had remained in her room, which was not like her at all.

"Red, can you check on Faith?"

"Will Beth still be breathing when I come back?" he asked.

I nodded. "Scout's honor."

"You were never a scout," he said. But he turned on his heel and did what I'd asked.

Miguel scowled at me. "You shouldn't make promises you can't keep."

Beth spun to look him in the eye. "I said I'm sorry."

"Might be enough for Sunday, but not for me," he said. "I want the cancellation ink. I won't be watched like I'm back at the Order."

My breath caught in my throat. I swallowed hard.

We never had a private moment within the Order. We were surveilled within an inch of our lives—and our lives depended on obedience as much as on the results of completing successful missions.

The position Miguel held within the Order ended up very different than Sunday's or my status. When the three of us had entered the Order, Miguel's magic had been different. He'd had super-hero-level strength. The Order had chosen not to train him as an assassin. They'd culled him from the general population. They'd unmade him, and reconstructed his magic to make him a chameleon.

To unravel a person's magic like that—to turn them into something else—it was a kind of torture. Years' worth. After which, they put him to work guarding the Order's most valuable assets.

If the watch they'd kept on Sunday and me was soul-killing, the surveillance of the chameleons would have been hellish.

"You want it now?" I asked. "The cancellation ink?"

He nodded.

I looked at Beth. "You bring your supplies?"

"In my pack."

"Do you have orders to use them for anything else invasive?" Miguel asked.

Beth shook her head. "No, but I wouldn't do it anyway."

"Will Malek know it when Miguel's tat is fixed?" I asked.

"It's not like he's got a master tracking board all lit up in front of him and one of the lights goes out. More like he feels—we feel—the vibe. And we get magical mental alerts. When that happens, whatever's happening comes to mind as if it were someone else's thought."

I knew how that felt. It happened to me all the time with *La Muerte.* "An absence of those thoughts from one of us might not alarm Malek right away, but over time?"

"Yes, that," she said. "Sunday, do you want the cancellation ink, too?"

Sunday mulled the question. "No."

No explanation, and nothing amounting to one showed in Sunday's expression. So Beth might not understand that beneath the 'no' lurked a desire for revenge. Sunday would get it, too. She'd never failed in all the years I'd known her. It didn't matter whether Malek was a god.

The ink was a potential weapon. Sunday would use it.

Miguel's mouth curved. He understood. And he'd be glad to let Sunday handle it on his behalf.

Beth looked from Miguel to Sunday to me, her forehead wrinkling. "Shouldn't Red be back by now?"

Yes, he should. With Faith in tow.

I marched for Faith's room, sliding around the dining table and past Red's and my bedroom into the hall. The door was wide open, every lamp in the space lit.

Small white desk with a simple oak chair against the near wall. Deep blue sea of a loveseat on the opposite wall, its armrest stacked with books to be read. Full-sized bed with sparkly gold satin comforter underneath the triple window on the far wall. Everything in its place except for the two people we'd been waiting for.

Red and Faith stood on top of the bed, feet slipping on the satin. They studied the window as if they'd never seen one before. They'd pulled the blinds all the way up. Ice crystals and condensation framed the glass. The sidewalk outside was clear.

My hackles rose. Faith and Red were exposed to anyone outside who wanted to see in.

I cleared my throat.

Red looked over his shoulder. "Do us a favor?"

"How about you do me one and tell me what's going on?"

He ignored my words and my worry. Faith didn't spare so much as a glance.

"Try to go outside," he said.

"What?"

"Walk out the front door," he said. "Someone. Anyone."

I raised my voice. "Sunday! Try leaving the apartment."

From the living room came the rhythm of her footfalls, followed by the soft squeal of the front door's hinges. Nothing after that—not for a long moment.

I stepped out of the bedroom to get a better look. Miguel and Beth stood side by side, their mouths hanging open. And Sunday had backed away from the threshold. She looked at it as if it were an alien.

"No?" I asked.

She shook her head. "Some kind of—I don't know—force field. I stepped out of the house. I swear I did. But I ended up right here, where I'm standing. I tried twice."

What the ever-loving fuck was going on? "Miguel?"

He didn't answer.

"Miguel!"

He turned to meet my gaze. His eyes looked haunted. "Is this the Order's doing?"

First the surveillance. Now the inability to leave. Sounded like. Felt like. But it wasn't the Order. It couldn't be.

"Beth?"

She shook her head. "I had nothing to do with this. Malek either. I'd know. I'd smell his blood in the magic. This is next-level. I've only ever seen this happen in the vicinity of a Horseman."

Not me, or the Horseman I carried. Not Luna or Pestilence, either. The fourth Horseman had yet to appear. Which, if Beth was right, left only one to blame.

CHAPTER 4

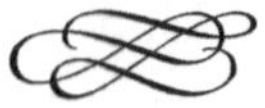

"FAMINE." Her name tasted like ashes in my mouth.

The apartment felt the same as it always had. The magical protections had given no warning of an intruder or tampering. Music flowed from the TV speakers. The world outside the windows looked exactly as it had when Miguel and Beth had walked through the door. Portland was a winter wonderland. The bare branches of the trees along the street clacked in the breeze.

Claustrophobia wanted to wrap its claws around my throat.

That feeling came over me suddenly, and from the outside. I'd never feared or felt uncomfortable in enclosed spaces, no matter how small. Someone wanted me to feel that way now.

Beth went rigid for a moment. Beside her, Miguel began to pace the length of the living room, his steps solid on the bamboo floor before softening on the rug. Sunday stood very still, fingers splayed.

From my vantage in the hall, I saw Faith cock her head. Red backpedaled from the window, hopping off the bed. He half-turned, looking at me, then trained his gaze on Faith. The sacred heart tattoo on his chest glowed bright enough to see not only light, but color through the fleece of his hoodie.

"Faith, what do you hear?" he asked.

She spoke so low, I barely heard. "A voice on the wind."

"What's it saying?"

"Something about strength and power against us. I can't make out the rest. The wind keeps eating the words."

My magic, not far beneath the surface since I'd first laid eyes on Mark in the coffee shop, surged in response to her words—and to the sounds carried on and muffled by the wind. I could barely make them out now that I knew they were there, the whisper faint and like nails on a chalkboard. The wings on my back vibrated and snapped open, the right wing punching through sheetrock. The other set of wings —*La Muerte's* wings inside of me, wrapped around my heart —fluttered.

Always a sign to pay attention. Half the time, a warning.

"Faith," I said. "Step away from the glass."

She made no move, as if she didn't hear me.

"Faith!"

My shout didn't appear to break her focus at all.

"Red, grab her."

He picked her up bodily from where she stood on the bed and dragged her away from the window. I waved him forward, forcing my wings to retract and backing up so that he could bring her into the living room, where Beth remained frozen and Miguel continued to pace.

Red laid Faith down on the floor near the dining table. She shook her head to clear it, climbing slowly and steadily out of the pit into which she'd dropped, thank all the powers.

Sunday's voice washed away my fleeting relief. "Night!"

I spun to find her arms wrapped around Beth.

"Something's got her," Sunday said.

Beth's eyes were unfocused, a vertical line forming in the center of her brow. Her lips moved, but nothing intelligible came out. I closed the distance between us, letting my hand fly for Beth's cheek. The slap rocked her head to the side. She didn't cry out or even flinch.

"Put her on the floor," I said.

Sunday swept Beth off her feet and knelt, lowering the girl to the rug.

I knelt in front of Beth, staving off panic with the ironclad presence of mind that came from my Order training.

Red crouched beside me. "What do you need?"

"I've got her. Watch the others. Help them."

He pushed away, leaving me the space I needed to extend my wings once again. I moved on instinct, without knowing why or how, only knowing what felt right.

I wrapped my wings around both Beth and me. They encircled us completely, magically expanding to seal off any sight, scent, light, or sound of the world outside. There was no floor. No ceiling. No one else.

My eyes adjusted to the darkness as if I'd been born to it. Sealing us off from the others—from the goddamn wind—changed nothing in Beth's affect.

My magic overflowed my skin, filling the bubble of air around us, spearing into Beth's mind, cutting through her shields like a buzz saw.

That triggered a magical alarm two thousand miles away. I felt Malek's attention turn toward Beth. He saw and felt what had happened to her even over the vast distance.

I didn't have time for Malek. Not to wait for him. Not to deal with him.

I plunged into Beth's waking mind and woven memories, coming to rest in a barren landscape, the land dead and brown. The soil I stood on broke beneath my feet. No moisture. No hope.

The air stank so badly of sulfur, my eyes burned. The sky was orange and black, as if it had been scorched, and the temperature hovered at freezing. Beth stood a short distance away, alone at the center of a crossroads. Tears stained her cheeks. She planted her feet on the crumbling ground, her hands curled into fists at her side, mouth open in a silent scream.

Across from her stood a ten-year-old girl with pigtails and tortoiseshell glasses. The kid wore a navy blue dress with red polka dots, red socks, and navy Mary Janes. She looked at Faith the way a budding psychopath might look at an animal it planned to kill.

I recognized her, having seen her once before in Houston, a couple of blocks from Malek's shop. The Horseman in me had recognized the Horseman in her—some fucked-up kind of Namaste. She'd only marked me with her eyes. She'd been watching at the time. Waiting.

The Angel wove his magic with mine. The ice of the grave. The weight of millennia. The mastery of death in its proper time and place. Sovereignty over the souls of the dead.

Our magic flowed from our skin, staining the sky. It flowed through the cold air like ink through water, forming great black wings that blotted out the light, casting a shadow and a pall over the Horse-woman Famine.

She met my gaze. "You can't kill me."

I didn't need to kill her. I only needed to hurt her.

She understood my intent without a spoken word. A glint of surprise shone in her eyes before she covered it up.

Did she think I was on her side? Without any proof, she did. We were made of the same stuff. We were sisters of a kind.

That was presumptuous and bullshit, and if she'd done an ounce of homework on me, she'd know it.

The Angel and I shoved our magic forward, the wings breaking into silent spears of smoke that streaked toward Famine. A rain of darkness. A rain of death.

Her fingers twitched.

In the space of a second, a portal opened behind her. She stepped back and let it swallow her before it closed and winked out of sight, stealing her away.

Just like that, she was gone.

The rain of magic pummeled empty space. The Angel and I arrested the magic's momentum, drawing the darkness back into ourselves. It flowed in through the pores of my skin, entering my bloodstream, riding the red current to my heart. There, the magic settled, the power of death mingled with the life force I carried, beating in time with my heartbeat.

Beth's scream found volume. "—bitch!"

The tail end of an insult meant for Famine, not me.

Beth lurched forward, catching her balance before she toppled, resting a trembling hand on my shoulder.

"Goddamn, Night."

"My thoughts, exactly. What happened?"

"I don't know. She's never done anything like that before."

"She knew where you would be. Or she has the ability to track you."

Beth swallowed hard. "Here's where you say, 'I told you so,' isn't it? Who'd have thought karma would bite me in the ass so soon?"

I shook my head. "I'm pissed at you, Beth. I don't want you destroyed."

"That makes me feel loads better."

"Don't relax on me yet," I said. "I'm gonna pull out of your mind now. Once I'm gone, you open your eyes. You communicate clearly that you're all right. Sunday laid you down on the floor. *La Muerte* and I have you surrounded."

I waited for a response.

After a moment, Beth nodded. She drew her hand away.

I slipped out of her mind, returning to my own consciousness piece by piece, heartbeat by heartbeat, to find myself in total darkness, cocooned by my physical wings. I couldn't see Beth's eyes, but I felt her gaze upon me, and the shuddering of her body as she breathed.

"Ready?" I asked.

"Please," she said.

On a steady breath, I unlocked the places where the feathers had expanded to seal Beth and me from the outside world, letting in streams of air and light and sound.

Red's muffled voice entered through the space I'd created. "Are you all right?"

I retracted the wings the rest of the way, drawing them tight against my back. The gray light of the overcast morning gleamed bright enough to hurt my eyes. I blinked until my sight adjusted. Until the living room and the people in it seemed as normal to me as the darkness had felt.

Red hunkered down across from me, on the other side of Beth. He met my gaze, his green eyes brimming with worry. Sweat beaded on his forehead. The sacred heart tattoo on his chest still glowed, although with a little less intensity.

"We're okay," I said.

He wiped his brow with his sleeve. "Jesus, Night. How did you do that?"

"Do what?"

"Your wings—they turned hard. Like stone. I couldn't get to you."

I stared at him.

"No joke," he said.

I could think about that later. How inexplicable it was. Whether it was dangerous. What it meant. "Can you take a look at Beth? Famine invaded her mind. Her magic. I want to make sure every trace of the Horsewoman is gone. That she didn't leave any booby traps behind."

"Hello?" Beth pushed up on her elbows. "Lying right here. Stop talking about me as if I'm somewhere else."

"Shut up and be still," I said.

Her eyes flashed with anger, but she did what I asked.

Red's grass-and-earth magic expanded to surround Beth, infiltrating her orange-and-black halo, burrowing beneath the skin. He took his time searching, a few minutes that felt like forever.

When he finally pulled away, he sighed. "No time bombs I can detect. No fragments of Famine. As far as I can tell, it's just Beth in there."

I squeezed his shoulder, then turned my head to meet Beth's gaze. "What did she do to you?"

"I can't describe it exactly," Beth said. "It felt like she was searching for something. Combing through my—I dunno—my blood? That makes me think it's about Malek, or my connection with him."

She held out her hands. I took one and Red grabbed the other. We helped her to sit up.

"She slithered in while the rest of you were trying to figure out what was happening," Beth said. "She pinned me to the place where I was standing. I literally couldn't move. She followed my blood straight to my heart, and she was in there, picking through my feelings."

The Angel knew, so I knew, that Famine's talents lay in determining what a person hungered for above all else—the one thing they couldn't live without. Then she gave it to them. It was always a trap. It always turned into that person's version of hell. That was who she was. What she was.

"She find what she was looking for?" I asked.

Beth shrugged. "No clue. You surprised her, coming in the way you did. I got the feeling she expected to have more time. She had me by the proverbial throat, too. She expected you to talk to her. Negotiate."

"Not while she was attacking you."

Beth nodded. "How was this different from the last time, when Pestilence possessed Luna? It was attacking her, and you negotiated."

I sat back on my heels. It was a fair question.

Sunday answered for me. "Pestilence hadn't yet chosen a side. Famine has. Besides, if she'd killed you, we'd get Malek to bring you back."

Beth rolled her eyes. "I'll take door number one. That's a decent reason. And I can't deny that having a boss with resurrection in his back pocket is a good thing. But I gotta ask: Have you ever died?"

I glanced over my shoulder at Sunday. She perched on the end of the coffee table. Miguel sat beside her. They both looked shaken.

Sunday frowned.

Beth looked at me. "You, Night? Any of you?"

The others didn't say a word.

I'd come within a literal heartbeat, but the Angel had saved me at the last possible second. The trauma of it—of everything I'd been through—still got to me when I thought about it. Still, it wasn't the same, and I wouldn't pretend it was.

"No," I said, for all of us.

Beth took a moment to meet everyone's gaze, looking to me at the end. "I'm not mortal like the rest of you—maybe closest to what Night and Faith have become. I've got karmic ties to Malek. Dying for me meant living the last moments of my agonizing and bloody death over and over again, my soul still tied to my body, while I waited for him to find me. And then I got to wait while he painstakingly healed my broken body and then shoved my screaming soul back inside. Not to mention processing all of that after the fact, while trying to remain a functioning human being fighting the good fight. Right? I mean, kudos to the bunch of you who'll just move on to your next destination when the time comes, but it doesn't work that way for me, resurrection in the back pocket or not."

I felt every word like a slap, which was what she wanted me to feel.

"Damn," Red said softly.

Beth nodded. "Yeah. So do what you gotta do, but don't take my immortality for granted."

"Okay," I said.

"No apology?"

I glared at her. "For saving your heart or your soul, or whatever Famine was after?"

She floated the ghost of a smile. "Never hurts to ask."

I rose to my feet, grabbing her hand to haul her upright.

She dusted off her backside. "This is bad. Generally, I mean. We've got Michael and the End and human signs of the Apocalypse, and now we've got Famine, too. Could it get—"

Sunday held up a hand. "Do not finish that question."

"—any worse?"

Sunday let the jinx lie. "How many run-ins with Famine have you had?"

"Numerous," Beth said.

"What did you see exactly when this sort of thing happened before?"

"Something swept Famine into a dimension she couldn't escape. She's a master of portals, so no small feat, right?"

Right. "How did she get out?"

"Don't know. I was already gone by then."

"You never found out who did it?" I asked.

"No," she said. "Believe me, I've tried. I used every trick in my book."

Miguel combed his hands through his dark hair. "Why am I thinking we're gonna find out, sooner rather than later?"

Beth tapped her index finger to her temple in response.

"You got your phone?" I asked.

She reached into her back pocket and plucked it free, raising a brow.

"You planning to text Malek and tell him you're alive, or should I?" I asked.

"He knows. He always knows."

"So?"

She raised the other brow.

"He's not just your boss. He's your friend," I said.

"Who thinks he's my father."

From the particular annoyed-yet-wistful way she said that, he wasn't the only one who thought so. "Text him."

"Is that an order?" she asked.

Red shook his head. "Don't be an asshole, Beth. Consider it the first of many things you'll do to make up for deceiving us."

She stared at him. "The first of many? Unlike your girlfriend, I apologized."

He folded his arms across his chest, which still hadn't stopped glowing.

After a minute, she blinked and looked away, grumbling. She marched to the door—and across the threshold—into the great outdoors, standing on the stoop with a view of the narrow courtyard between apartment buildings. "Hey, check it out. We can leave if we want to."

Miguel relaxed, his shoulders dropping to their normal height.

Beth started to shut the door behind her.

"Nope," he said. "Keeping an eye on you. Anyway, what do you need privacy for? It's not like you're calling him."

She couldn't call Malek—he could hear her voice, but he wouldn't be able to use his own. He hadn't been able to speak since he'd left the Garden. The End had cursed him, taking away his tempting, velvet voice. Malek spoke only through sign language or writing.

Beth gave Miguel the side-eye and leaned against the outside wall, fingers moving. Her eyes took on a suspicious shine.

I cocked my head, an invitation for Miguel to come stand by me. He could keep an eye on Beth from over here. If she wanted—or needed—to cry with a sliver of privacy, we should let her.

He sidled up beside me. "More kindness than she deserves."

"One, just because she's lied doesn't mean I'm going to treat her the same way. Two, she really will make it up to us."

Beth stepped inside again, kicking the door closed with her heel. "How?"

"I'll decide how and when," I said.

She paused, taking in my meaning. "That won't work for me. My allegiance is to Malek."

"Whose orders you disobeyed, and who is probably just glad you're alive."

"True on both counts," she said. "But that doesn't mean there won't be a price. There's always a price. Blood and pain, like I said before."

I said nothing. This was not a negotiation.

"Shit," she said.

I knew how she felt. She was seventeen going on grown-up, and she looked like a cornered animal. She'd made decisions, and she'd have to live with the consequences. That was how life worked.

"If you're committing to our team—if you want to fight with us—then we have to live with your decisions, too," I said.

She frowned. "I know."

"Your word," I said.

She considered the choice. After a moment, she said, "You have it. My word."

Faith blew out a long breath. "Now that that's settled, can we talk about how Famine breached the protections?"

Beth raised a hand like a schoolgirl in class. "My fault, most likely. I can't be one-hundred-percent sure without a magical mental post-mortem—no offense, Night, but I'm okay to wait on having your magic inside my head again. Chances are, Famine had her hooks in me before I walked through your door. Before I ran into Miguel, even.

If she found a way to slip in and hide herself well enough, I probably carried her right in. That make sense?"

I nodded. The protections were strong enough in ordinary circumstances, but rudimentary, given that we hadn't spent much time here.

Miguel shook his head—not disagreeing, just disgusted. "You're counting too much on your reputation and skill to keep the peace around here. Neither of those things means jack shit to the level of bad guy we're dealing with now."

Red shoved his hands into the pockets of his hoodie. "That's harsh."

Sunday shrugged. "Not if it's true."

"I put up protections in the first place to stave off attacks from Order operatives," I said. "Those spells were never meant as an end-all, be-all. They were gonna catch ninety-nine percent of would-be assailants—knock them out or knock them down. Either way, we'd have early warning. Time to wake up if we were sleeping. Time to spin up our magic and grab a weapon. Famine is not an Order operative. For that matter, neither is Michael or Gabriel."

"Or the poor, unsuspecting people the End has somehow turned into signs of the Apocalypse," Faith said.

Miguel snapped his fingers. "Them, too. We need to step up our game."

Crafting the kinds of protections he was talking about would take time, which we didn't have. I opened my mouth to say so, but Miguel interrupted me.

"I know, Night. I know. I say we give Faith here a free hand with adding some oomph before we head out."

Faith tugged at the hem of her sweater. "Me?"

"You're the one with the god, aren't you?"

"That's not his specialty," she said.

Not to mention that Faith had no training in that area. "I'll do it."

"You did the ones that didn't work," Miguel said.

"*We'll* do it. The Angel and I."

"Right," he said. "That'll take care of the oomph."

I nodded. "We ready to go?"

Red shook his head. "Five minutes."

"What takes five minutes?" Beth asked.

"The microwave." He spun and headed into the kitchen. The crackle of a paper sack and the crinkle of aluminum foil followed.

Heating up the breakfast and coffee. Giving the rest of us time to gather our thoughts and, in Red's, Faith's, and my case, a change of clothes and a toothbrush. Miguel banked the fire and secured the screen, moving anything possibly flammable far out of the way and crossing himself when it was all said and done.

I'd never known him to be religious. None of us were. Any faith we'd had before the Order had been smothered by the mentors, by the training. No room for gods or grace or damnation in the assassin's soul.

I crouched beside him. "You mean all of that—what you said earlier?"

"About wanting out?"

"You didn't say that explicitly, but I got that was what you meant."

He nodded.

Part of me wanted to demand to know where this had come from. He'd fought with us. Never once breathed a word like this. Never even hinted at it. But the rest of me understood that going up against beings powerful enough to be gods meant an early grave and no chance to reclaim any part of who we'd once been.

If I could get out, would I?

If it meant spending the rest of my life growing old with Red and buying whatever children Faith might have one day—if she chose to do so—ridiculous gifts that only their *abuelita* would give? If I could see that as a viable choice? I'd be right behind Miguel.

"You planning to leave?" I asked.

"Nope. I'm with you."

"For how long?"

He didn't hesitate. "As long as you need me."

"I'm relieved," I said, and I meant it wholeheartedly.

He flashed a ghost of a smile. "You need me."

We did, but it went beyond that. Miguel was my friend, and I didn't have very many of those. Miguel understood me in ways that only one other—Sunday—could. The three of us were a team. We needed him, sure. But it was personal, too.

"I do," I said.

He reached out a hand and squeezed my shoulder, pushing to his feet and walking away before I could say anything else that might make him feel uncomfortable. After a moment, I followed his lead.

By the time we made our way outside, the sun had begun to melt the ice that it touched.

Everyone except Red and I headed down the salted concrete steps that led to the street, Sunday hauling our bags.

Red stood behind me, helping me to slide on my backpack before pulling on his coat as the Angel and I wove our magic once again. Doors were made to pass through, a purpose that always tried to reassert itself no matter the locks and bars engaged, physical or magical. Warding a door was harder than warding walls, and to really keep someone or something out, we had to go big or go home.

La Muerte and I marked the door with a series of symbols invisible to the non-magical, naked eye. The symbols looked the way our magic had inside of Beth's mind, like ink dispersing through water. They served as a warning—but also as a first strike. Anyone with ill intent who tried to enter the apartment would forget why they'd come and be compelled to leave.

It should work in full against any Order operative or Horseman. Archangels, to a lesser extent, but we couldn't have everything we wanted, could we?

As the Angel and I drew the last symbol, the ink of our magic spread to coat the walls and windows. To cover the exterior of the apartment. We waited until it felt right. Only then did we turn around.

I met Red's gaze, focusing on the lines etched around his eyes and noticing that his hair contained considerably more salt these days. Uncertainty filled his heart.

"You all right?" I asked.

He took my hand. His felt warm—mine were freezing.

"Am I all right?" he asked. "What about you? That was a little harrowing for straight out of the gate on a Sunday morning."

"It was ballsy as hell, what Famine did," I said.

"You're gonna make her pay?"

I nodded. "Soon as I get my hands on her."

He showed me a wry grin. He hadn't yet zipped his coat. He held a black knit hat in one fist. The glow of his sacred heart tattoo through the fabric of his hoodie was barely perceptible now.

I laid my free hand on his chest. If his hands felt warm, his chest felt hot.

"Yeah, that," he said. "I don't know what to make of it."

"It just is," I said. "Like the Angel."

"I'm not sure I can be philosophical about it, Night. Not when I'm shining like a neon sign."

I tilted my head, granting him the point. "How's it feel?"

"Like my heart could explode any minute."

I narrowed my eyes.

"Not my physical heart," he said. "The emotional one."

"I need to say something."

"Say away."

"Doubt's a bastard, Red. Don't let it take root."

He took in the words on a long breath, then drew me close to kiss the crown of my head. "Maybe Addie will have some information for us when we get there. She's been looking into this…whatever it is."

Changing the subject was a bastard, too.

I breathed in the grass and earth of his magic. "Let's hope."

The phone in my back pocket buzzed. I pulled away from Red to check it.

"What is it?" Red asked.

"Addie." I read her message twice. "We've got more unexpected company."

The Angel's wings fluttered beside my heart.

CHAPTER 5

EVERY MINUTE of the drive to Addie's pissed me off. The slip of the tires on ice, chains notwithstanding. The cramped quarters, with all of us squeezed into Sunday's stolen car. The sweat beading at my hairline as the full-blast heat and the combined body warmth made the air feel close and thick.

I imagined my phone had vibrated no less than five times. Each time I checked, neither Addie nor anyone else had sent messages.

Piling out of the car into the cold again sent a shock through my body. I drew a deep breath as Sunday and Miguel took automatic position at my flanks—as if this was a combat situation. The air smelled of firewood burning and snow. The only sound other than the drip of melting ice was a child's shriek a couple of blocks over, followed a heartbeat later by a gaggle of laughter.

I saw no one out of place. No one lying in wait.

We started up the deiced sidewalk and steps in a wedge, followed by Faith. Red and Beth brought up the rear. Icicles hung from the eaves of the two-story yellow house. All of the curtains had been thrown wide, the bottoms of the windows fogged. The rosemary and lavender hedges on the incline of Addie's yard had been buried underneath a frozen blanket. I brushed my hands along the edges, activating the rosemary's scent. Drawing it in steadied me.

The wide porch held a couple of rocking chairs with a small table in between. The chair closest to the door was taken by the big black-and-white tomcat who liked to hang around the place. In the other sat Stacy, our witch and the unexpected guest.

I wanted to think of her as—what had Miguel called Beth?—a friendly. But whatever else Stacy was, she belonged to Malek, too.

A fuchsia knit cap warmed her head, a riot of blond curls trailing past her shoulders. She wore a puffy, charcoal-gray down coat with matching mittens, a gray sweater with bright pink polka dots, and a bright pink skirt that flared at her ankles. No one would ever miss that girl. She practically glowed in the dark.

She raised a hand to wave.

I waved back. "Why're you here?"

"No hello? No small talk?" She sighed. "I came through the portal."

The secure magical path constructed between Stacy's and Beth's home base in Houston and ours in Portland, at the gym Red owned. Justice Gym was closed today on account of the weather. No one there to see her arrive. No one there to lock up after she left.

The hand wave was back. "I took care of the door. Don't worry about anyone breaking in. It'll open for the team, but no one else. Malek sent me. Said you would need me. Honestly, I'm glad to be here, even if we're all going to die."

I wanted to be angry with her the way I was with Beth. I wanted to be mad, period.

Miguel's words about getting out had shaken me. I hadn't expected them to. I'd taken on a destiny when I'd taken on the Angel. I'd more than resigned myself to that—I'd embraced it. It was a chance to do something good in the world. Something that would save lives—and balance the scales for me, wash away some of the blood on my hands.

I still wanted that. I needed it, and so did the world. So, why did I feel knocked off balance?

I shook it off and met Stacy's blue gaze. Her eyes had darkened since I'd seen her last to match her indigo halo.

"Why are you sitting on the porch?" I asked.

"Addie's in a bad mood. She had plans today, I guess."

"Plans?" I'd never known Addie to have a busy calendar, but then I'd only known Addie since the world had literally begun sliding into hell in a handbasket.

"A date," Stacy said.

I raised a brow.

"I know," she said. "It's kind of great. But anyway, she's pissed, and she's banging around in the kitchen, cooking for me. Chicken soup with matzo balls. Said they'll taste just like my grandmother's."

"I didn't know you were Jewish," I said.

"Learn something new every day. She's really not okay, Night. I don't know how to talk to her, but you do."

Addie and I had a truce these days—we'd had to work together to save each other and the people we loved too many times for us to be enemies, but she'd still put out a contract on my life when I'd been a child. She still thought I was too dangerous, and frankly I felt the same about her.

Stacy pushed up from the rocker and wrapped me in her arms, giving me a solid pat on the back before she pulled away.

I startled.

She flushed when she saw my expression. "Sorry."

"Most people don't hug me."

"They're afraid you'll shred them?" she asked.

Sunday laughed. "She will."

Stacy gave me a look that said she knew better.

I stepped past her and the cat, leaving the rest of the team to be greeted and hugged as they preferred. I hope Sunday got the extra edition.

Addie's living room smelled like heaven, if heaven were chicken soup—and like anger, as if the air itself were burning.

The house spirit met me there, a formless light and force of protection and blessing with the well-being of the house and all people whom Addie welcomed as its mission. It looked me over, sniffed me over, and brushed the nape of my neck as it recognized me and granted its approval.

The place felt normal. No magical disruptions that I could detect. It was the safest place I knew. And I knew there was no such thing as safe.

The space had shed all of its Christmas glory except a single string of clear lights to the right on the mantle, woven around a line of family photos. A little light to drive out the darkness.

A fire burned in the hearth, wood crackling behind a wrought iron grate as if it were hatching a plot to escape its prison. Matching light brown sofas squared off against each other, the coffee table in the middle serving as referee. On the left, the formal dining table that never saw any use—all the action happened at the kitchen table, the beating heart of the house. Which was where I'd find Addie.

I toed off my boots and hung my coat on the tree by the door, taking the well-worn path across the oak floorboards to the kitchen. Addie leaned against the counter beside the coffee maker, sipping the dregs from a mug the size of the Empire State Building. She wore her hair in the usual bun, secured this morning with a chopstick that looked as if it'd been plucked from the silverware drawer. Her dark brown skin shone with the heat of the kitchen and a powder keg of pent-up emotion.

Her halo might as well have been the Milky Way, festooned with so many stars, I could hardly see the black velvet around them. I couldn't tell whether the stars were about to implode or explode. Maybe both.

Behind the silver-wire frames of her glasses, her dark brown eyes lit up, and not with happiness. She wore a pair of black leggings and a purple long-sleeved shirt emblazoned with a litany of goodness— from "In this house, immigrants are welcome" to "Love wins."

She set down the mug with a bang. "About time."

I ignored that. There was nothing to be done about the apocalyptic circumstances, or the weather, or how long it had taken us to get here.

The chairs around the old oak table at the far end of the room held the usual suspects, all of them with their lips zipped, and all of them sitting still as statues, as if moving meant incurring wrath.

Jess, Addie's niece, had taken the spot at the end near the back door. She had her aunt's dark brown eyes and wore her hair in the same bun, her ears barren of her favorite gold hoops. Her halo looked like Addie's, too—in her case, a night sky spiraling with stars. Jess was a Watcher, too. She didn't have Addie's training. To get it, she'd have to leave to study with the oldest Watchers, and they'd thrown their power in this battle to the End. They were our enemies.

Jess still had on last night's yellow rubber ducky pajamas, her feet tucked into matching fuzzy socks. At the sight of me, she hugged her knees to her chest and leaned back, tilting her chair against the windowsill behind her.

Her boyfriend, Ben, sat beside her, wrapped in a long-sleeved T-shirt and jeans the same color as his strong, stone-gray halo. The ends of his brown hair were still damp and his white cheeks were flushed from the shower. His long bangs concealed one brown eye.

He spoke in an uncertain baritone. "Night, how was New Year's?"

"Uneventful," I said.

On the other side of him, the third usual suspect sat, resplendent in black and white from her sweater to her tights. She wore skull cameos in her ears, around her neck, and on her fingers. Her fire-engine-red bob shone under the kitchen light. Her bone-white halo shone, too. Corey, Faith's girlfriend.

Behind me, Faith entered the kitchen. She slipped around the far side of the table and took the chair beside Corey's.

The others piled in, filling the room with riled magic and growling stomachs. Miguel and Red crowded at my sides. Sunday wound her way around us.

Addie met their eyes one by one, her gaze coming to rest on mine. Stacy was right. She was most definitely not okay.

"I don't know what I was thinking, enjoying having the house to myself," she said.

Jess cleared her throat. Of all of us, she was the one who was supposed to live here.

"Mostly to myself," Addie corrected. "This feels more normal. More comfortable. Heaven help me. I know Stacy has a plan."

Sunday moved to stand in front of the stove, leaning to peer into the simmering pot of soup. "Can we talk about that over soup?"

"Should be about ready," Addie said. "Stacy gets the first bowl. And we should eat in the front room. Some of us can take a seat on the sofas and use the coffee table. The rest of us can sit at the dining table."

"When was the last time someone actually ate there?" Sunday asked.

"Ten years ago. When my husband was still alive and I still had a family," Addie said, then corrected herself before Jess could protest. "A bigger family."

Sunday turned to meet her gaze, surprised.

"I had a life before you all showed up on my doorstep," Addie said. "I'm still trying to have one."

Sunday backed away from both the stove and the conversation.

Jess stood, chair legs scraping the tile. "You want me to grab the extra plates and bowls from the basement?"

Addie nodded. "Sunday can help you."

Sunday's gaze brushed mine, a clear desire to object written on her face. But she kept her mouth shut and followed Jess into the hall. The basement door squealed on its hinges a moment later. The click of chain that lit the bare bulb over the basement stairs followed.

"Everybody out," Addie said. "Go sit down. Night and Red will help me with the bowls."

Miguel arched a brow. He leaned toward me, muttering, "Just once, I'd like to be a fly on the wall."

"No, you wouldn't," Addie said.

Miguel took the same tack as Sunday, foregoing a reply. Instead, he led the march from the kitchen into the front room, leaving Red and me with Addie.

"There's soup spoons in the drawer behind me, Mr. Jennings." Addie pushed away from the counter to give him access and closed the distance between us.

"What's up?" I asked.

"I don't know." After a moment, she said, "That's not entirely true. It's my husband's birthday, just so you know. I'm sure Stacy told you I had a date?"

"She did."

"It's with him."

"Symbolically or for real?" I asked.

There was magic, and then there was Watcher magic, which could create and destroy. Addie could unravel the fabric of the universe commensurate with the level of her power, which was less than some but a lot more than people gave her credit for. She could weave life into the universe the same way.

"It shouldn't matter," she said, sadness painting her words. "But it's for real. It's a ritual we do every year. His spirit travels here and we have a chance to be together again. He can never stay long. Couple of days, then he's gone again."

I didn't have to work hard to imagine how that might feel. If Red were taken from me—I tried not to think too hard about that, because there were no guarantees. If I had a chance to see him, even for a little while, it would be the most important thing I did.

"You want us to handle this on our own?" I asked. "We can set up somewhere else. Call you if we need you."

Addie shook her head. "I'm not bowing out."

"But—"

"No buts," she said. "I didn't tell you so you'd feel sorry for me, or so you'd go away. I just need you to know why I'm so short with everyone. That's probably not going to change too much. I just don't have the energy to pretend I'm okay."

"Understood," I said.

Red pulled every soup spoon from the drawer. All of that metal clinked in his hands. "What do you need from us?"

"Discretion," she said. "I don't want to hear about this from any of the others. If I think of something else, I'll ask."

"All right," he said.

She rubbed her forehead with her fingertips. "Night, what do you know about the signs of the Apocalypse?"

"Only what I've read or seen in movies," I said. "It's not a topic of discussion at the Order—or it wasn't while I was there."

"And the Angel?" she asked.

"He's been silent on the subject."

"Good reason for that, I suppose. They change, depending on the circumstances."

Red stared at her before recovering with sarcasm. "Of course they do. Why wouldn't they? Jesus."

He walked the spoons out to the waiting crowd.

Addie tried on a smile. It didn't quite reach her eyes. "He's a good one, Night."

"I know."

"Don't let him get into too much trouble. And don't let him go."

"No," I said.

"You notice anything different about the man you ran into this morning? The one who was possessed?"

"He had the End's halo. Empty and cold."

"Anything else?"

I shook my head.

"There had to have been a clue about what he was up to," she said. "You just didn't know what to look for."

"Probable," I said. "I've never seen something like that before, and I don't have any previous training in sign-spotting. I'm wondering about the Angel."

"What he's not saying? Don't worry about it."

"Why not?"

"If he had something to say at this point, he'd offer it," she said. "You two are together in this all the way. It's not just the wings. Your halo is being rewired."

I hadn't noticed. Then again, I hadn't wanted to.

Not everyone could see halos. It'd slipped my mind that Watchers could do so. And that Addie and Jess would've been watching me every bit as closely as I watched our enemies, because of the Angel.

"What do you see?" I asked.

"It's very subtle. Your halo is black. His is black. There's not the same color weave that's happened with Faith or Beth."

Faith and the Awakened. Beth and the serpent.

"It's more shades of gray with you and the Angel of Death," Addie said. "I can make out striations. Shapes. And…eyes. Your halo has begun to look less like one solid sheet of black and more like a collection of black wings, as if it's made of a million birds."

"You can't be serious," I said.

"Deadly."

"Blackbirds?"

"Crows. Ravens. I don't know. That part seems less important than the part where it's not exactly a human halo any longer. It's a—for lack of a better word—hybrid."

I didn't know what to say. I didn't know how to feel, either. "Why are you telling me this now?"

"Because someone should," she said. "And because it means something. That you and the Angel are becoming one being, drawing closer each day—but it's more than that. There are always multiple meanings for any one thing, the same way that each of us is a multifaceted being. What we mean to every person in our lives is different. Am I making sense?"

"I think so," I said.

"Let that be enough for now. The ladies are on their way up with the bowls we need."

I caught the creak of a stair or two as they ascended from the basement a split second later.

Addie read a spark of surprise on my face—not that she'd heard the creak, but that she'd heard it before I had.

"It's my house," she said. "I've lived here longer than you. But it's not just that."

"The house spirit?"

She flashed a wry smile. "You keep thinking of that spirit as if it's a discrete entity. A separate being from the house itself."

I'd thought just that. "It *is* the house."

"It is," she said. "And it's my house."

I returned her grin as Jess and Sunday walked by on their way to join the others. "I've never heard anyone call Sunday a lady before."

"Don't tell her I did that. I'll never hear the end of it."

Truer words.

Beth, Jess, and Ben took the dining table. Miguel made a place beside the fire. The rest of us settled on the sofas.

By the time we were all situated in the front room, slurping bowls of heaven, the sun had moved into the space, stretching through the window glass like a languid animal across the oak floor. The last of the icicles had melted from the first floor eaves. The branches of the trees glittered, the occasional crack sounding as ice broke from the bark and splintered against the sidewalk and the street.

"So," Beth said. "What's the plan?"

Addie set down her bowl of soup on the coffee table. She glanced at Sunday, who sat beside her, then at Red and me on the sofa opposite, before she answered. "First, we figure out who the End has possessed. I'd like to work with Stacy on that."

The witch nodded.

"This isn't the first time the world has ended. The first time, it was water," Addie said.

"The proverbial flood." Miguel sipped his soup directly from the bowl.

"That's right." Addie rested her chin atop steepled fingers. "The next ending—the one we're trying to prevent—is apocalypse by fire."

"Nuclear?" he asked.

"It's possible," Addie said. "But my bet is on something magical. Someone magical. That gives us is a clue as to what kinds of signs to look for. Who is the End possessing? Are they all ordinary humans? If they are, who are they connected to? What are they tasked with doing?"

"The logical place to start is to find those with fire-related magic in the city," I said. "Once you and Addie find them, we can track them."

"I can rig the spell so that we can stake them out from here," Stacy said. "Not just their movements—where they are, where they're headed—but what's actually happening to them, moment to moment. How they're feeling about it. What they're planning to do."

Sunday tucked her legs underneath her butt and pushed up taller on her sofa cushion. "You want to hack their minds?"

"Exactly," Stacy said.

Sunday's lips curved. "I like you."

"Is this a variant on the spell we did when we invaded the Order?" I asked.

We'd joined as one, with everyone's magic accessible to me. It had been powerful. It had enabled the Angel and I to wound the End badly enough to win.

Stacy grinned. "It is."

I stood up. "What are the materials you need?"

"There's a list." Stacy rose as well, digging into the side pocket of her skirt to produce a folded slip of paper. "We probably have most of this."

I reached for the list and passed it to Addie. She looked it over, sliding her finger down paper's edge until she came to the last item. "Everything but this. White angel feather? You didn't need this the last time."

Stacy shifted her weight from one foot to the other. "Like Night said, it's a variant, not an identical casting. This one incorporates an angelic component. More oomph and, well, illumination."

"I have angel feathers," I said.

"Your—the collective your—power's not about lighting up secrets, Night."

No, it wasn't. We could compel the souls of the dead and shepherd them to their next destination. We had power over death, not light. "The angels who have that power are not our friends."

"They're not our enemies, either. Michael said—"

Beth interrupted. "She knows what Michael said. She was there, Stacy. You and I got the eavesdroppers' version."

Stacy's eyes widened. "She knows already?"

"They all know."

Stacy met my gaze. "I was about to tell you."

I folded my arms across my chest.

Stacy took a deep breath. "Michael helped us just by showing up. By telling you what's going on."

"Then he told me he'd have to be hands-off," I said.

"If he won't give you a feather, ask Gabriel."

Gabriel, who spent his time flitting all over the world, granting magic to unsuspecting normals in an attempt to balance the scales of the final battle. No care for what that magic did to them, or whether their bodies, minds, or souls could handle it.

"You're shitting me," Red said.

My feelings exactly.

Stacy shrugged. "You use the resources you have. He's a resource."

I glanced at Addie. Out of all of us, she and I were the only ones who'd successfully summoned an angel. She was hurting, and my first impulse was to take the task on myself without asking her. But not asking would only piss her off more.

She sighed. "Stacy, set up the spell in the basement. Night, what do you think? Which one do we ask?"

"I think it has to be Michael," I said. "I'm not willing to risk the lives and souls of every normal in the vicinity, and that's what it would come down to with Gabriel."

After a moment, she said, "There are others, you know."

"A million angels dancing on the head of a pin, somewhere out there?"

"Archangels," she said. "And more like a handful."

We knew Michael and Gabriel, insofar as anyone could "know" an archangel. There were others out there, sure. But they were mysteries. Unknown quantities. And in one case—Lucifer's—notorious.

I shook my head. "No, thanks. Not unless we have to."

"Okay," she said. "I can perform the summoning. We'll bring him here, like last time."

When she'd called him to the house and he'd given me an ultimatum. His way or the highway. Good times.

I opened my mouth to answer, but a voice rang in my head. The words died on my tongue.

CHAPTER 6

THE VOICE SOUNDED nothing like *La Muerte*'s. It bore no resemblance to the voice of Luna's soul either, which had once resided in the recesses of my heart but no longer abided there. The one word it spoke bled power that wanted to bend every thought racing through my head and every breath of air that filled my lungs.

The sound was so big, I felt as if my head might explode. As in, full-blown blood and brains all over Addie's nice oak floor. I recognized the particular combination of annoyance and authority.

Michael.

Go outside and walk south, he said.

The fuck are you doing in my head?

Helping.

After telling me he wasn't allowed to intervene. After disappearing in front of me on the street without answering all of my questions. *I'm not dreaming. How are you in my head?*

Like your friend Miguel said, you need to work on your protections.

My personal protections had always served. I'd never had my shields breached without my permission.

I blinked, my vision blurring. I'd developed layers of personal protection against attack during my time at the Order, and after I'd left I'd added shields against scrying or spying to the best of my ability. I'd been the Order's second best, right behind Sunday.

There was always someone better—smarter, faster, stronger. That was life. But I was damn powerful. I wasn't an archangel. I didn't know—yet—how to keep one out of my head. Michael had come to me in dreams, but never before while I was awake.

He was right. I'd have to find a way to bolster my protections.

I'm helping, he said again.

I'd be the judge of that. *Turn down the volume.*

He did. A little. *Is that better?*

Enough so that my head might remain intact. *Prove that you're who you say you are.*

That I'm not a chameleon?

Woe upon the chameleon who had the balls to copy Michael—but it could happen. "Yes."

He showed me something that only the two of us could know about. The dream in which he'd come to tell me that the children inside the Order were dying, and why. He'd shown me the moment the Order had come for me, down the street from the smoldering ruin of my parents' house, while frogs sang in the shallow overgrown ditches on either side of the road. He'd shown me how that moment had played out for Sunday, and for Miguel. For every single magical child the Order had ever preyed upon under the guise of giving us somewhere to belong.

The whole dream replayed in the space of a heartbeat, and I understood the ring of truth in it. This was Michael, not someone who'd co-opted his characteristics and magic.

He gifted me with one other thing: his coming to me in that dream was not sanctioned. It wasn't that he couldn't help me now; he was never supposed to help at all. But he had. I wasn't sure how I felt about that.

Decide later, he said. *Listen here and now.*

Here and now. *What's south?*

The man you let go this morning. He's still possessed.

It should've been impossible—I'd looked into the man's mind. I hadn't seen anything suspicious. Then again, I hadn't done a thorough examination because Michael's presence across the street startled me.

And that was an excuse. Whether or not it was a good excuse didn't matter, only the result. If Mark was south of here, I needed to find him.

Will I need the car?

Go on foot.

How much time do I have?

Go now.

I blinked again, my vision clearing to show I'd walked halfway to the front door already, and worried faces all around. Beth and Stacy, glancing at each other. Ben reaching for Jess's hand. Corey's face, as bone-white as her magic. And Faith, pushing to her feet, her eyes glowing with the same silver and gold woven in her halo.

Red stood behind me, his hands settling on my hips. "What happened?"

I lifted his hands and turned to look at him. "I need to take a walk."

I headed for the front door, grabbing my boots and catching sight of Jess from the corner of my eye as she rose from her seat and headed upstairs, taking the steps two at a time.

Red followed me, placing himself between me and the door. "What's going on?"

"Michael," I said.

"Where?"

"In my head."

"How?"

"I don't know. He's bigger and more powerful than I am and he found a way in." I shoved one foot into its boot and then the other, bending to pull them on.

Red frowned. "Is he making you do this?"

I glared at him. "No one can make me do anything."

As the words flowed off my tongue, I wondered if I lied. I had no real idea what feats of magical might Michael could or could not perform. Maybe he could overpower me. Maybe he could compel me. The important thing at the moment? He wasn't.

"You trust him all of a sudden?" Red asked. "After everything that's happened?

A complicated question with a simple answer. "No. But I believe what he's telling me. Mark is close. We need to get him off the street."

I filled them in as I finished tying my shoes.

Faith closed the distance to us. The silver-and-gold glow in her eyes and halo translated to sparks that dripped from her fingertips. "What do we do?"

"We go with her," Red said.

Sunday shook her head. "Miguel and I will go. And you, Red. Your magic might come in handy. Everyone else stays for now."

Faith narrowed her eyes. "You can't make that decision for us."

"It's not about emotions, Faith. It's about strategy. I need the rest of you to stay here and prepare the basement to hold this guy. We need to get him off the street so that he can't hurt anyone else."

"Maybe he's not trying to hurt anyone," Faith said.

Sunday shrugged. "I'm not willing to take that chance. We get him off the street and into the best containment we can build. Then we question him until we get the answers we need. Understand?"

Faith looked from Sunday to me, then back again, fear in her eyes.

Sunday held her gaze. "I'm not going to let anything happen to your mom. Trust me."

"I do," Faith said. "But it might not be enough."

"I'll keep her safe or die trying," Sunday said.

After that, it was a flurry of coats and boots. Jess ran down the stairs, hands full of black elastic bands wrapped with silver coils.

"Like tire chains, but for your feet," she said.

She tried to hand a pair to Sunday, but she produced a set from her coat pocket—always prepared. The rest of us slipped ours on. We were going to need them.

Last thing, I slipped on my backpack. We stepped out once more into the icy air.

A shiver rolled through me, starting at the balls of my feet and crashing like a wave through the crown of my head. The street remained as deserted as it'd been when we pulled up. The kids had gone inside, leaving the neighborhood as silent as death. Even with the smoke drifting from chimneys and the occasional light shining from a bare window, the street felt apocalyptically empty, as if the world had turned on its head.

No one watched us from the houses. No one spied on us from behind a parked car. No magical tendrils traced the air. No itch at the back of my neck. Ergo, no ambush. But the whole thing felt wrong.

I turned my head to look at Sunday. "You feel that?"

"I don't like it," she said.

Miguel nodded. "But we're going anyway."

Red slipped a knit hat from his coat pocket and pulled it on. "Someone has spelled the block. Maybe the whole neighborhood."

I stared at him.

"It's subtle," he said. "Like a veil. One made from fabric so thin, you wouldn't know it's there unless you looked in the right place."

"I looked," I said.

"Uh-huh—outside. Look inward."

I turned my magic toward myself. My eyes. My mind. My heart. And caught an infinitesimal something. A wisp of a shadow.

"The hell?"

"I know, right?" Red shook his head as if to clear it. "I can't tell what it's designed to do."

I could. It was my job to know and see these things, it was just that usually I knew and saw them in other people's halos. The spell had been spread thin, all right. At first blush, it looked colorless, but closer examination showed a misty gray and a yellow that tasted of hunger.

"What does it feel like to you, Sunday?" I asked.

She hesitated. "Like glory. Like I've finally won every battle. Like I can rest now."

Miguel chimed in, his words flavored with desire. "It's a scent. Clean air. Heat on the wind. Grass seed. Animals. Seasoned wood."

Red's hint of a drawl deepened. "It feels like you, Night."

"It's Famine," I said.

Sunday spat on the porch.

My feelings exactly. I focused my attention and my magic on the veil, hunting for that wisp of a shadow I'd seen originally—there. I tightened my grip on it and tugged. It fell like rain from a pregnant cloud, sliding out of mind and heart and dousing the wood at my feet with a solid, yellow splat that vanished a half-second after it struck.

The block didn't look or feel any different, but I felt clear-headed, the strange upside-down feeling gone.

I glanced at Sunday. "Let me in?"

She nodded.

It took a good few minutes to clear her and the others.

"Maybe we should bring Ben," Miguel said. "He could shield us from this kind of crap."

Sunday took point on the way down Addie's steps. "He could also get himself in trouble or killed. This is not just about Mark anymore. This is another Horseman we're talking about. She's hit us twice already and the day isn't even over yet. I'm not taking that kid into a fight unless I have no other choice."

Miguel didn't answer because there was no good answer to Sunday's point.

Michael's voice bloomed in my mind.

"Michael says hang a left, go to the end of the block, then left again."

We did what he asked, heading west.

I felt a tug on the heart link that Red and I shared. It was about more than the bond between us. He was using his magic to monitor the state of my heart and magic. It was a safeguard—he'd see any further spell-driven alterations in me.

There was something else, though. He more than monitored—he was rooting around. Looking for something.

I met his gaze. "What are you doing?"

"Looking for threads between you and Sunday. Between you and Miguel. It could come in useful."

"Later," I said.

He shook his head. "We're just walking."

"No such thing when you're headed for a threat."

We reached the end of the block and took the second left onto the shaded side of the street. The shoe chains performed like champs. My feet didn't slip, not even an inch. Without the sun's kiss, the ice and snow held on tightly to the concrete and grass and the tops of the rhododendrons planted on the side of the corner house. The house's looming shadow reminded me inexplicably of a child's closet monster.

I hadn't thought of the closet monster since before my parents died. The rhododendrons seemed to grow taller, as if they were adults and I was only a little girl. Their broad leaves, curled against the snow, rattled as the wind picked up. The current carried with it childhood scents. *Posole.* Auto grease. My mother's rose perfume.

Red tugged on the heart link. He was rooting around again, but this time not to explore my connections with the others. This time, he worked to dispel the sensory input—the sensory overwhelm—of magic thrown at me.

It felt nothing like the End's power, and everything like Famine's.

The spell this morning that had frozen Beth and trapped the rest of us in the apartment could've been done from afar and with forethought. The overlay of foreboding and hunger that had been cast upon the neighborhood block and on all of us could've been done from afar and set to trigger as soon as we left Addie's house. But this casting could only have been done by someone nearby.

Famine had eyes on us.

Far ahead—three, four blocks—this street intersected Broadway. If people were out and about, they'd be there, patronizing whatever restaurants, bars, coffee shops, or stores had managed to open.

Twenty feet ahead, a familiar bearded guy in a green knit cap and matching coat. Jeans and hiking boots. Pale white skin, the lenses of his silver-wire-framed glasses casting shadows beneath his eyes. The corners of his mouth turned down, trembling. The absence of a halo, a negative. He watched the sidewalk in front of him, feet sliding on the slick surface.

Red stopped in his tracks, dropping behind the rest of us. That would keep him out of the way and give him a good vantage point if he needed to act.

Michael's voice and the Angel's sounded in my mind, ringing over each other and reverberating in my bones.

Take care, Michael said. *He has enough of the End in him to do you harm.*

La Muerte's words were fewer, and filled with concern. *Don't let him touch you.*

I repeated the warnings to the others under my breath. Miguel tightened his hands into fists for a brief moment. Sunday widened her stance.

I stepped out in front of her, brushing close as I did. "Famine's here."

She nodded, turning to Miguel and leaving me to address our enemy number one.

I raised a hand to wave. "Mark."

He looked up to meet my gaze. There was something wrong with his face, easier to see when he looked at me. Bags under his eyes for days—no, his eyes seemed sunken. Cheekbones, now sharp as razors. Lines at the corners of his mouth looked like seams, as if his expression were stitched together. Or as if it were coming apart.

Mark was human. He was carrying a piece of the End inside him. That couldn't be good for him. It might be worse than bad—it might be fatal if it went on long enough.

His voice sounded normal. Everyday. Nothing sinister there. It was a lie.

"I was hoping I'd find you here."

"Here I am. I brought friends."

He sighed. "You think you're going to take me—"

Miguel's purple bruise of a halo flashed dark and bright. He launched himself at Mark, heedless of the warnings I'd conveyed. At the same instant, Sunday threw her blinding magic at the man.

Mark's eyes glazed, unfocused. He didn't act like most people on the other end of Sunday's power—he didn't panic. Instead, he raised his hands in the direction of Miguel's attack.

Miguel shifted his trajectory at the last second, rolling low and sweeping Mark's legs. Mark went down in a blind heap.

I wanted to slide my magic into his mind. The Angel's and my power combined might be enough to make him compliant or immobilize him. But bending all our will and magic toward him meant none to spare for Famine. And it would leave Red vulnerable.

"Sunday, can you hold him?"

She nodded. "Got him."

Michael raised his voice inside my head. *She doesn't have him. It's beyond her ability.*

"Left back pocket," Sunday said to Miguel.

Miguel reached in and plucked out a set of zip ties. He and Sunday managed to yank Mark's hands behind him and to bind him.

Too simple. Too easy.

My vision seized on a pinhole in the house's closet-monster shadow, the faintest shaft of light. The stench of sulfur followed, staining the nearby snow yellow as the pinhole widened into a full-fledged portal. Famine stepped from sulfurous light into the icy shade, at first little-girl-sized, but growing twice as big, as if she'd imbibed an Alice in Wonderland potion.

Her eyes were like saucers. All black, no pupil, behind her tortoise-shell glasses. The wind ruffled the hem of her navy blue dress and picked up her pigtails. She grinned at me, a hellish diversion as the struggle among Mark, Sunday, and Miguel grew suddenly louder and more violent.

The Angel's and my gathered magic licked the inside edges of my skin. The wings around my heart fluttered against my ribs. Our magic screamed at me to attack, but we'd gone after her full-bore inside Beth's mind. She'd gotten a taste of our magic. She'd be prepared for an all-out assault.

Her gray-and-yellow halo simmered. "What are you waiting for?"

A tendril of yellow and gray drifted from her halo, snaking toward me—then veering sharply toward my flank. And Red.

I spun to face him. His gaze grazed my face, our eyes meeting in a flash before he locked eyes with Famine. He gasped at what he saw— her heart? Her incoming strike? He didn't bother to dodge or run.

I screamed his name.

Famine's mouth curved into a Cheshire grin.

The tendril wrapped around his legs and wound up his body, caging him in and seeking his heart. It took no time at all. She would have him. Take him. Hurt him.

The tattoo on his chest flared, its light disintegrating the magic.

Famine's jaw dropped.

Red shot me a look from the corner of his eye that said *I've got her.*

Despite his power being new and relatively untested. Despite the nature of the fight. Despite everything.

I let go of my fear for him. The Angel and I turned toward the others.

Mark had wrenched himself from Sunday's and Miguel's grasp, eyes still unfocused and glazed—still blind. He'd snapped the zip-ties binding his wrists. He stood on the balls of his feet, expecting another physical attack. He didn't expect the Angel and me.

Our magic poured from the pores of our skin in jets of smoke and ice-cold death, plunging toward him so fast, Sunday and Miguel barely had time to dive out of the way.

Mark's head swiveled toward us a moment before the magic hit him. He grunted in pain and his legs gave way, his knees striking the concrete with a crack.

The inside of his mind was agony. The lightning pain of the fall. The scream of his psyche completely overwhelmed by the End. The cold beyond life and time that the End brought with him everywhere he went. The kind that killed and shattered everything in its presence.

It invaded the surface of my skin, turning it to ice. It slid between cells and molecules, freezing into a lacework as it flowed. It sank deep into my bones and took the marrow hostage under a cover of frost. I couldn't breathe. I couldn't taste. My body numbed.

We'd been here before, the Angel and I. We'd wounded the End badly enough to send him away. He'd gone to ground. We thought he'd hidden whole and alone somewhere only he could find, licking his wounds and plotting his next move. But he'd split himself into parts and possessed the people who would become signs of the Apocalypse. And now he'd come here, to my city—into the neighborhood where my family lived. Seeking us out.

Seeking you out, Michael said, his voice so faint I almost missed it.

Mark—the End—growled.

The Angel and I froze his voice. We froze his movements. We held him still because we could. If all of the End had been within Mark, we might not have been able to, but because the End had split himself into pieces, we forced him to obey.

"You'll come with us," the Angel and I said, our voices harmonizing.

Sunday spoke. Her words sounded far away. "Night, Famine's gone. She ran from Red."

I only liked the sound of that on the surface. She was gone? Great. Red was all right? Thank all the powers. But Famine had never run from anyone or anything that I knew of. Retreated, sure.

"Let's get this guy back to the house," the Angel and I said.

Miguel sounded uneasy. "Pronto. There's a cop down at Broadway and he's looking our direction."

I followed his gaze to mark the officer at the corner. If he'd glanced our way, he'd shifted his attention. "How long did he look this way?"

"Handful of seconds."

"Long enough."

"Exactly."

I gave Miguel a quick once-over. "You feel any different after laying hands on Mark?"

Miguel shook his head.

"Sunday?"

"No," she said. "I got your warning loud and clear, but nothing happened. At least not yet."

The Angel and I let off the magical throttle enough to allow Mark to move his legs. "Sunday and Miguel, help him walk. Be careful."

Miguel opened his mouth, then snapped it shut. Asking me how to be careful when I had no idea was counterproductive.

Instead, he and Sunday raised Mark's arms and ducked underneath, as if Mark was a friend who'd sprained an ankle while navigating the ice. If the cop or anyone else took another look, they'd see friends helping one of their own.

The Angel and I kept our focus on Mark and the End, but I stepped toward Red and offered my hand. He twined his fingers with mine, and we swept in behind the others.

Heat flowed off of him—no doubt the glow of his tattoo gave off enough thermal energy to warm him up like that. He gripped my hand extra tight. No wonder there. He'd gone toe-to-toe with a Horseman.

"What just happened?" he asked.

"We got ambushed. We could've had our asses handed to us. I thought there were enough of us."

"We should've brought Beth," he said. "Or Addie."

"I agree. But you did—I don't know what you did. It was amazing."

"I just stood there," he said. "The magic moved through me and stopped hers."

"She's hate and hunger." I squeezed his hand. "You're love and compassion."

"Matter and anti-matter?"

"Opposites."

"Does that make me her mortal enemy?" he asked.

"Probably." We rounded the corner onto Addie's street. "Is Famine's veil still operative? Or is it—"

"Gone," he said. "Michael?"

"I haven't heard a word from him since the Angel and I got a hold on Mark. My head no longer feels like a grape about to be squished."

"So, gone."

I nodded.

"You seem fine," he said. "As in, not frozen to death. That's different than the last time you locked minds with the End."

I hadn't noticed, which felt more than a little unsettling. The Angel and I had encountered the unbearable cold, but after that, the pain and discomfort faded. Because we were only dealing with part of the End? Or because something else had shifted for me as the Angel and I grew closer?

I didn't know what to say, so I went with nothing.

The sound of footfalls and the shine of an orange-and-black halo announced Beth's presence on the walk in front of us before I laid eyes on her. She skidded and slid to a stop in front of us, out of breath. She set her hands on her hips, then thought better of it when her footing began to falter.

I met her gaze, then inclined my head toward Sunday, Miguel, and Mark. "Let them pass."

Beth stepped onto the lawn behind her, frozen grass crunching under foot. "Where is she?"

Meaning Famine.

"She fled before my superior magical firepower," Red said.

Beth stared at him.

He frowned.

She took in his expression, then chanced another step toward the corner, leaning forward to get a better look at considerable peril. "There's a cop coming this way."

Either our friends-helping-friends ruse hadn't convinced him or there was something else going on. I saw no halo or lack thereof. Bottom line, though, he was dangerous. He was police.

"Can you deal with him?" I asked.

"I'll make him go away," she said. "The last thing we need is police in the middle of a magical crisis."

There were other considerations. "Magic will protect itself. It always does. The last thing we need is police at a house filled with black and brown people."

She took that in and rolled up her sleeves, baring tattooed glyphs. No doubt, one of them held persuasion magic.

Red and I left her to handle the problem, quickening our pace to catch up with the others. We climbed the stairs through the rosemary and lavender and melting snow to Addie's porch. She stood at the threshold, her halo a glory of shooting stars and novas.

She gave Mark the once-over. "Basement's ready."

Red tightened his grasp on my hand for a long moment, then let go, following our quarry into the house. The Angel's and my work of holding on to Mark grew a little easier in the presence of the house spirit, as if it lent us its powers of containment and order.

Addie glanced past me. "Where's Beth?"

"Handling a human threat."

I watched her face as she processed the possibilities. It wouldn't be one of the neighbors. They knew Addie, and they'd gotten used to the sight of the rest of us over the last few months.

"One with a badge?" she asked.

I nodded.

She sighed. "Come on in. I'm not paying to heat the neighborhood. Beth will find her way back."

By the time I reached the bottom of the basement stairs and passed through the layers of magical protections set into the foundation and the walls, Sunday and Miguel had secured Mark to a chair in the center of the space with more zip ties and an ample amount of duct tape. They'd pulled off Mark's hikers. He curled his bare toes into the red rug and scanned the circle of many-colored pillows around him. He didn't show an ounce of fear.

The End had nothing to be afraid of. No natural enemies that could overwhelm him completely. The only reason we could hold him at all was because we weren't dealing with all of him.

No illusions, no mistakes.

Sunday had taken up station near the door on the far side of the basement that led out to the side yard. Miguel leaned against the side of the stairs, ready in case trouble presented itself from that avenue. The kids had settled along the wall between them, leaning on or sitting on top of the washer and dryer, all eyes on the prisoner.

While we were out, Stacy had built something truly impressive from the combined magic of those who'd remained behind. Around the circle of pillows and Mark/the End in the chair at its center, Stacy had crafted a magical shield. On the inside, it had been bolstered into unbreakable status by Addie's and Jess's Watcher power. On the outside, it had been covered with a thin layer of Faith's silver-and-gold explosive magic and sealed with an orange-and-black safety net, along with a drop of Beth's poisonous blood.

If it wouldn't hold Mark and the piece of the End he carried, it would hurt them.

Stacy was nowhere to be seen. Upstairs somewhere, then.

I wagged a finger in Faith's direction.

She hopped off her dryer perch and made her way over.

"Tell me about the explosive," I said.

She leaned into me. "It's anti-magic, not anti-human. Ben and Jess told me what happened before. I don't want anyone else innocent to…"

I finished the sentence for her. "Die here."

Luna had perished twice in the spot where our prisoner sat. It had been horrible for her to go through and horrible for the rest of us to watch, helpless to do anything.

"The safety net?" I asked.

"So we don't blow up. And we don't blow up Addie's house."

"Good thinking," I said. "Stacy is…?"

"Here." Stacy ducked through the shields, fortified with a portion of all the magic she'd woven. Her hair looked like spun gold. Her skin glowed with life and light. Her indigo halo spiraled with black streaks. "Red and Addie are waiting upstairs for Beth. And keeping watch. Are you sure it's a good idea to bring him here? He's inside our safe space."

"No such thing," I said.

She rolled her eyes. "You know what I mean."

Of course I did. "I'm not being a wiseass. I have a good reason for wanting him in here."

"When are you planning to share?" she asked.

Not right now. Not within Mark's and the End's earshot, which right now probably encompassed the entire house.

Stacy wasn't the only one with questions about what I had up my sleeve. He might not have said anything since his final warning back on the street, but the starry presence of Michael's mind remained within mine, and he was definitely not comfortable.

"Do you trust me?" I asked aloud, as much of him as of Stacy.

She nodded without hesitation. From Michael, not so much as a flicker.

"Good," I said. "Reach for me magically."

She cocked her head. "We have the circle."

"In case it's not enough."

She hesitated a second, then sent her power toward me. The Angel and I reached out and grabbed it, drawing it inside, close to the heart.

"Ready now?" she asked.

As I'd ever be. I turned on my heel and closed the distance to the prisoner, sealing myself inside the circle with him. I could see and hear the others just fine, even if their voices came through muffled.

I shrugged out of my backpack and tossed it out of the way. The coat followed, thrown into a heap atop the canvas and leather. I stretched my wings to full capacity and got to work.

CHAPTER 7

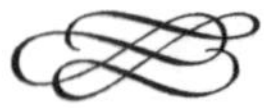

MARK GRIMACED at me, sweat beginning to dampen the brown hair at his temples. He looked as if he wanted to rub his palms along his thighs, but having his hands taped to the chair prevented that kind of nervous gesture. The eyes behind his silver-wire-framed glasses looked stunned, as if he'd awakened from a nightmare and discovered it hadn't been a dream after all. He looked worse than he had outside, as if the deterioration were accelerating.

"You're the woman. From the sidewalk. From outside the taqueria," he said.

I didn't sense the End in those words. Either the End had released Mark—unlikely—or he'd let go just enough to allow Mark to use his senses and his voice. Mark would be disoriented. Confused.

"Why am I tied up?"

"A precaution," I said.

Mark blinked, seeming to truly see me for a moment. "Why do you have wings? The fuck are you?"

"I should ask the same thing of you," I said.

"What's that mean?"

"You know you're not the only one in there, right? There's another consciousness inside your head."

"That's fucking nuts," he said.

"It's called possession."

"Possession? What the—wait, *possession?*"

I nodded.

"That's only in movies."

I took a couple of steps toward him, lowering myself into a crouch so I could meet his gaze on his level. "I'm sorry this is happening to you."

"Then let me go."

The Angel and I tightened our hold on him, slipping more deeply into his mind. I saw everything that had been there before, from the moment Mark woke this morning to his brush with the neighbor that had stolen his consciousness. I lingered there, showing him that moment, not as he preferred to remember it, but as a calculated move on the part of the being who'd possessed his neighbor.

The instinctive parts of him understood some of what had happened.

The fine nurse in her pink scrubs, red hair pulled into a ponytail at the nape of her neck and freckles washed across her nose. She'd marked him with her sleepy brown eyes and shifted the angle of her walk so that she would brush against him. The sort of action that could be bundled in with flirting—an accidental run-in—or could be explained away by fatigue or a simple inability to walk in a straight line when preoccupied. Powers knew plenty of people had that problem.

He'd missed the fine web of magic that arced across the surface of her body, of her clothes and hair, because he didn't have the magic, the knowledge, or the training to see it and know it for what it was: a sign of viral magic.

People didn't use that kind of magic often. It had a high chance of backfiring on its host—keeping the virus alive and contained drained all of the host's life force, and passing it on to the intended target killed the host seventy-five percent of the time. But the End wasn't a person, and as far as I knew its life force was inexhaustible.

When that woman touched Mark, a zing had coiled through his

body, like the feeling he got when he picked up someone else's static electricity. The taste of ashes filled his mouth, so much so that he'd actually spat into the bushes at the end of the walk. That hadn't helped much, so he'd decided on the coffee shop.

He lowered his exhausted self into the car and shut the door, closing out the strange static neighbor thing along with the rest of the world, exchanging that for silence and floating dust motes. His windshield began to fog from the heat of his breath and body. He punched the brake with his foot and pushed the start button and then, before he could set his hands on the wheel, his vision started to fuzz from the inside out, like a month-old tomato in the back of the fridge.

The fuzz turned to sludge, and the sludge poured through his head from back to front, edging out his senses until he could no longer hear or taste or see. The feeling in his skin was the last thing to go.

Was he having a stroke? Was this what dying felt like?

Yes, the End said to him.

The only word spoken between them.

Mark's heart raced. Sweat popped out along his forehead.

And then there was nothing at all.

I slid apart from the memory, allowing Mark's human consciousness just enough space to recognize what I'd shown him.

Mark had no web of viral magic on him. Either he was the terminus—the one the magic had been sent to find in the first place—or he was somehow incapable of passing it on, like a human black hole, taking in what was sent his way but unable to get rid of it.

Either way, he was fucked. It wasn't right. It wasn't fair. It made me want to scream. The silence between us felt loud and thick, with mass and weight.

After a moment, his small voice echoed. *What is that thing?*

It's the end of all things, I said. *It's sunk a claw into you and I need to know why. If you know, you should tell me. I can help you.*

Mark wanted to believe that more than he'd ever wanted to believe anything. But I had big black wings and I was responsible for tying him to a chair in an unfamiliar basement, so he didn't trust me.

I'm all you've got. My friends and I.

He mulled that for a long minute. *I'm just a guy. I don't have any special knowledge that anyone would want. I'm good with numbers. I'm a bookkeeper. But none of the money I keep track of is mine. Why would anyone want to...possess...me?*

No lie there, only genuine bewilderment. Poor bastard.

The faintest sound rose from the depths of Mark's mind, like an exhalation, followed by the stillness between breaths. It was the sort of sound that anyone would miss, part of the natural rhythm of firing synapses and mental images and ricocheting thoughts.

The set of the spring before a trap snaps shut.

The magical threads of the End's trap shimmered into being inside Mark's mind, cracking like whips as they drove toward the Angel's and my presence there. Ready to lock down. Ready to annihilate.

The End's consciousness overwhelmed Mark's. Its thoughts tasted like ashes, its tone filled with contempt.

Stupid for someone so smart.

Stupid to think I could fool a being that ancient and powerful. To think I could slip out of the trap at the last second, with the End vulnerable for having overreached. The End could summon any or all of the humans who'd been infected by him. Who carried parts of him within themselves. They could be here in minutes. The End would destroy us. All of us.

The litany of thoughts was a distraction in itself. An attempt to focus my attention and magic on the sound of them instead of on the shape of the trap.

The Angel's voice rang. Not in my mind, but in my heart. *Now.*

We reached—not for escape, but for the trap itself. Our magical hands closed around its threads from the inside. We yanked them toward us with lightning speed.

Ice froze our fingers in place, the frost descending, taking over every inch, every cell, every molecule of our magic in Mark's mind and of my physical body. I ignored the howling pain that overtook my flesh and blood. The only thing that mattered was in the threads of the End's magic.

The piece of the End's consciousness that resided in Mark descended to cover ours.

La Muerte and I could hear what the End heard, see what he saw. Mark as a human man—only human, an imperfect and stinking animal—with blood on his hands.

Before his seemingly perfect life, he'd lived something much more difficult. Abandoned at birth, and then by a series of foster parents until he aged out of the system. He'd built layer upon protective layer of psychic bandages over the wounds he carried, but sometimes they bled through, coppery and slick and raw. And when they did, he became screaming-, punching-through-walls-, and sometimes people-punching-and-bone-crunching violent, but most his violence was self-directed and self-destructive, alcohol his drug of choice. The taste of blended Scotch never strayed far from his memory, no matter what he did to distract himself or how far he thought he'd come. It hounded him. Haunted him.

An ice-blue flame of despair rose like a dragon rearing on its hind legs, huge and looming with undeniable power, jaws wide open to deliver cleansing fire. Any minute, the fatal rush would come. Any second now.

Every second, every day of his life.

Mark was no different than too many others, scarred from experience and barely hanging on. Abandonment issues, anxiety, and using copious amounts of alcohol to numb heart- and mind-rending pain was an understandable, if harmful, reaction. That he'd managed to make a good life for himself and trust enough to have a relationship was downright heroic.

Mark wasn't a sign of the apocalypse. He was a sign of humanity.

The End had steered him into my neighborhood for a reason, and that reason was me. The End wanted to get to me. Put some kind of spell on me, maybe. Or pummel me to dust by presenting person after possessed person for me to save. I'd feel compelled to rescue every one of them, but there'd be no way I could.

Or was it something else?

If it was, I couldn't see it, and neither could the Angel.

Michael sighed, the sound a light against growing hopelessness and dread. *Break the trap now.*

The Angel and I tightened our grip on the End's threads. In the space and power of a heartbeat, we tore them to shreds. The pieces disintegrated. All of them. The icy fire of despair flared, trying to hold on, then flickered once, twice, three times before it snuffed out, wisps of smoke rising like ghosts and fading away.

La Muerte and I waited a long moment, just to be sure, before we slipped carefully from Mark's mind, consciousness settling into my cold, trembling body. The Angel's power moved through me in a wave, stealing the death from my form, allowing warmth to enter.

I blinked frost-coated lashes, clearing my vision. The basement rushed in—the yellow and green and blue pillows, the blue rug, the in-the-crosshairs feeling of all eyes on me. Everything outside the inner circle Stacy and the others had built remained blurry.

I focused on Mark. Was he still a danger? My gut said no.

I met his hollowed-out gaze, smudges beneath his eyes deep and heavy, as if he'd been dipped in the fires of his own hell and scorched to the marrow. I released the magical hold on him slowly, allowing him to get a feel for his body gradually. I didn't want to shock him any more than I needed to.

He opened his mouth to speak, but sucked in a breath instead, on the edge of hyperventilating.

Addie's footfalls on the concrete widened my focus beyond him. The basement outside the circle began to come into view, like grains of sand sifting through an hourglass, the smallest pieces combining to create the whole.

I locked eyes with Sunday, still standing watch at the side door with an uncharacteristic tension in her shoulders and a vertical line bisecting her brow. She asked a question with her eyes. Was the business with Mark and the End handled?

I nodded.

She rolled her shoulders, but the line remained.

Addie stepped into the inner circle behind Mark, a red wool blanket in her hands. She wrapped it around his shoulders.

He flinched.

She set her hands on his shoulders. "You can let go of all that fear for now."

He reacted automatically. "I'm not—"

She leaned forward, flashing him a look that quelled the lie. Of course he was scared. This shit wasn't some kind of everyday adult thing you bluffed your way through. Mark was a normal. This was magic with cosmic stakes.

He searched for different words and spat them out. "I'm pissed."

"You should be," she said. "I'd be out of here already if I were you."

"I can't do that, can I? You people tied me to a chair."

"For your own good."

"That's only partially true," Sunday said.

Mark turned his head to look at her.

"It was also for our safety," she said. "You were dangerous. My friend with the wings says you're not anymore."

"I don't know what that means. I don't want to know."

"Try to relax," she said. "We're not going to hurt you."

He seemed to believe her. "Was that real? Please tell me it wasn't real."

"Sorry," she said.

"That's it?"

"That's it."

He took another deep breath and shuddered as he exhaled.

Addie knelt and held out her hand. I reached for my knife and gave it to her to cut the man loose. He rubbed his forearms, then rested his head in his hands.

He didn't run. Instead, he looked at me through the space between his fingers. "I should be long gone. I should call the cops. I should call my therapist and ask for an emergency appointment."

Putting myself in his shoes, I'd feel the same. "Why aren't you?"

"I haven't made up my mind," he said.

"About?"

"I need the facts. I need you to tell me what the fuck's going on. Spell out what just happened to me—all of it. I learned a long time ago that pretending won't make something go away, or turn it into something it's not." He combed his fingers through his hair. "I'm angry. And, yeah, I'm scared. What if it happens again? What if I don't know what to do to protect myself?"

I silently filled in the last questions, the ones he didn't ask aloud, but that I could see racing behind his eyes. I'd been inside his mind. I knew what he feared most.

What if there was nothing he could do, and he was at the mercy of people or things with the power to control him? What if he did something terrible while under that control?

He'd done terrible things before under the sway of a substance that he was addicted to. He understood what had just happened to him much more deeply than he could possible guess.

"I've already told you," I said.

"That I was possessed. By who?" He glanced from my face to my wings and back again.

"He who wants the world to end."

Mark's eyes filled with horror and confusion. I wished there was something I could do for him, to make it easier to accept the facts he'd asked for. I could read his thoughts and feelings. I could control him.

"If you want to forget any of this ever happened, I can help you do that," I said.

He shook his head.

"It's a trauma. You shouldn't have to carry it."

He shook his head again, this time with force. "I shouldn't have to carry a lot of things. No—no one is going to gaslight me. No one's going to leave me with the strange feeling that something happened I can't put my finger on or leave me wondering what's wrong with me. That's how it works. That's how it always works."

I stared at him. "Someone has altered your memories before?"

"Not like you can," he said. "Doesn't matter how you do it, it always works out wrong."

I held up both hands to reassure. "Okay."

He studied me, deciding whether to believe what I'd said. "Okay."

"Would you take heart's ease?" I asked.

"You can do that?"

"Not me," I said. Easing hearts was Red's territory. I glanced over my shoulder, to make sure he hadn't taken up position behind me. He wasn't there.

I rose, drawing my wings tight against my back. "Addie, can you take over here?"

"Sure," she said. "Last I saw, Red was in the kitchen."

I flashed her a wry smile before heading out of the inner circle, slipping past Stacy, my gaze grazing the kids before coming to rest on Miguel, who leaned against the stair wall, one foot on the floor and one braced against the sheetrock, arms folded across his chest.

"You watch him?" I asked.

His bruised halo flared. "We've got him."

I turned to leave the basement protections behind, catching Mark's low question and Addie's answer before I stepped through to the stair landing.

"What is she?" Mark asked.

Addie was matter-of-fact. "No one you want to mess with."

"What. Is. She?"

"The Angel of Death," Miguel said.

The words twisted inside me, all of my human parts—everything in me that was Night Sanchez—crying out in protest.

I took a deep breath, white-knuckling the bannister, and climbed the steps like a prisoner of darkness heading towards the blessed light. I felt that way for exactly the time it took to reach the basement door and shut it behind me on protesting hinges.

Afternoon light penetrated from the front windows into the hall, setting the oak floor aglow and illuminating dust motes that floated past my face. I expected to hear the clink of cups or glasses from the kitchen. I expected to hear Red answering Beth's typical embarrassing questions in a frustrated, exaggerated drawl. Instead, all I heard was the ticking of the kitchen clock and the small sighs of the settling house. My hackles rose.

I tugged on the heart link with Red. He answered with a warning from the front porch. Not an announcement of danger, but a clear push to stay away.

I reached out with my magic, seeking a glimpse of him and whoever —or whatever—had captured his attention out there. It flowed through spaces between the weatherstrip and the doorjamb, sliding over Red and Beth and the solitary cop whom Beth had said she'd handle.

Whatever she'd planned to do hadn't worked, or it hadn't worked the way she'd counted on. She had powerful magic at her disposal. She should've been able to send the officer on his way, no problem.

I knocked on the door of her mind. She let me in, her thoughts and feelings rushing into me like a raging flood. She was pissed off and frustrated and frightened.

I swam to the top of the roaring stream of mind and emotion to find the loudest, most important information: the cop was immune to her power.

I sucked in a breath.

Magic protected itself. Normals didn't notice it, period—possessed people like Mark aside. So the cop not knowing magic exists, not seeing it, not feeling it? Sure. But immunity? I'd never heard of such a thing.

What are you talking about with him? I asked.

Shooting the shit and trying to figure out what the hell he wants. He says he's just checking on folks, but he won't leave. This is super strange and Red can't help because his chest might start glowing again and then we'd be in serious trouble and I don't know what to do you got any ideas?

I let my magic flow toward the officer, testing his edges and tasting his halo and finding something other than the normal shine of basic human life force. His halo was a creamy light brown. Beneath that, quicksilver, intoxicating and invigorating and not human at all. Neither Red nor Beth had noticed.

He's fae, I said.

Beth sent me the thought equivalent of a shocked stare. *I should be able to tell that. Why can't I tell that?*

He's camouflaged. Doesn't want you to know.

Kevin wouldn't send this guy, she said.

Kevin, the once-human Faery King. Not the usual Faery regent, and new to his throne.

Faery was a big realm with as many political factions as the human world. What were the odds that every fae being was happy about Kevin's ascension? What were the odds that they would just go along with a former human taking the throne?

I slammed on the thought-brakes.

Where had that line of thinking come from? Not from me. And not from anyone to whom I'd magically connected. I didn't give a damn about fae politics. Kevin could handle his own problems. If he needed help, he knew how to get in touch.

They were the Angel's thoughts, his mind woven with mine so seamlessly in the moment that I hadn't been able to tell the difference.

If I'd felt twisted before, now the discomfort multiplied. I pushed it away.

Beth's voice echoed in my mind. *Wow, that's intense.*

She'd heard every word. Caught every nuance.

So what do we do? she asked.

My first impulse was to step outside, but that could go wrong in a hundred different ways.

Hold tight, I said.

I slipped my magic through the fae cop's café-latte-and-quicksilver halo and into his mind, finding only minor magical shielding that yielded to my power with an audible thump that reminded me of the sound a body made under the wheels of a car.

He felt me there. Felt the fist of my magic tighten around his mind.

The Angel's initial thoughts had hit a bull's-eye. This guy was no friend of Kevin Landon's. He'd been sent to gather intel on Kevin's friends with orders to engage in conversation, not violence. His guise as a cop was nothing new—the previous Faery King sent messengers and spies who wore the uniforms of human law enforcement officers, the better to force cooperation and obedience.

This guy had come here to spy. He'd spent powers knew how long shooting the shit with an embodiment of the Sacred Heart and the apprentice to the Serpent on the porch of a house belonging to a descendant of fallen angels. He had to know what he was getting himself into. Whom he might encounter.

Who sent you? I asked.

He didn't answer.

I tightened my magical grasp on him, rifling through his thoughts until I found an image that would answer for him. A fae woman dressed all in white—a wedding dress?—with brown eyes as old as time, raven hair, and lips red as roses. She spoke with someone more familiar. Someone who looked like a little girl, but whose saucer eyes behind tortoiseshell glasses were all malevolence and greed.

Famine. Fan-fucking-tastic.

Who is the woman in white? I asked.

I can't speak her name, the spy cop said.

Not that he wouldn't. He literally couldn't. A spell prevented him from doing so.

Leave now, I said. *Don't come back.*

Or?

I said nothing. No need to complete the threat.

He shivered within my grasp.

I let him go.

He stepped sideways. With a flash of light and a whiff of sulfur, he vanished into the In-Between.

Beth glared at the spot where he'd stood for a full minute before turning on her heel and marching back in to the house, Red right behind her. I pulled back my magic, sliding out of her mind and meeting her gaze as Red closed the front door and threw the deadbolt, locking out the rest of the world.

"I hope that motherfucker gets lost," she said.

It was possible these days. The In-Between had been shifting for a while, becoming less and less reliable as a way to move between worlds.

"What do you know?" I asked.

Beth showed me an exaggerated shrug. "That cop—that fae spy— the fae woman he serves is working with Famine. You warned him not to come back, but he's totally coming back. Or his friends are. Don't we already have enough to deal with? Famine. The End. Michael. I mean, where does it stop?"

Red held up a hand. "Hey, Beth. Calm down."

She wheeled on him. "You're joking, right? Calm down? When did telling a woman to calm down ever come across well?"

He backpedaled a step.

"I don't know," I said.

Beth narrowed her eyes. "What do you mean?"

"I don't know where it stops, or when it stops, or if it stops." A dull ache settled in the center of my forehead. I rubbed it with the heel of my hand. "Who's the woman in white?"

She snapped her mouth shut.

I volunteered more information. "Wedding dress? Fae?"

"Classified," she said.

"You're joking."

She shook her head. "I've already dug myself a hole with Malek. I'm not willing to dig all the way to China."

Telling me that was the same as giving me more information. I raised a brow.

She blanched and changed the subject. "You have a plan, right? For the End and everything?"

I let my hand fall. "No."

"But you always have a plan."

"Where have you been all this time, Beth? Were you paying attention? I'm winging it."

"Pun intended?"

I stared at her.

"Well, let's hope and pray it doesn't get any worse," she said.

A knock on the door shook the painted steel in its frame.

Red raised a brow. "You were saying?"

She turned to look at him. "That's not fair."

"Fair's on Sunday out in the country." His gaze brushed mine as he braced himself to answer the knock.

He pulled open the door not to a fae horde or a Horseman or an archangel, but to a short, stocky woman in a blue denim shirt, khakis, and white sneakers, wearing no coat or sweater against the cold.

Her halo shone like the moon over smooth, dark water. It did more than reflect the flavor of her life force and her magic; it carried a hush so profound that for the space of a breath, I imagined I could hear the soft lap of water against a distant shore and the faint hum of insects as they hovered over the surface, gazing at their own reflections.

I'd seen and felt my *abuelita* in memories, but never in living color a few feet away—at least, not that I remembered. The trauma of my childhood and the Order's training had wiped away so much, so many pieces of my past that still remained a mystery to me.

Dream looked exactly as she had in my memories, only bigger—and smaller. A force of nature wrapped in the form of a human woman.

She'd pulled her long, dark hair into a loose bun at the crown of her head, escaped strands curling around her brown face. Her brown eyes contained the wisdom of the ages. She trained them on me.

"*Buenas tardes, nena.* You planning to invite me in?"

"Who're you?" Beth asked.

"Night's and Miguel's grandmother, Dream," Red answered. "Come on in. Whether or not you can stay is up to the house spirit and the woman who owns the place."

"Addie and I are friendly," Dream said.

Beth sighed. "Well, thank God. We've had nothing but enemies all day."

Dream stepped inside. The house spirit took her measure, and it didn't throw her out. It didn't seem to know what to do with her at all, actually, except to hover.

I knew how it felt. What the hell was Dream doing at my front door? What was she doing striding toward me, wrapping me in her arms as if I were long-lost family? People did not hug me. Elder beings most especially did not hug me. Above all things, they didn't make me feel as if I were a child again.

I breathed her in. She smelled of sand and the salt of the sea, wrapped around a core of warmth and strength. She planted a kiss on my cheek and one on my brow, shooing away the headache before it had a chance to sink its claws too deeply.

She drew back, clasping my shoulders and shaking me gently. "You're in trouble."

It took a minute to make my voice work properly. "You come to help me with that?"

She cocked her head. "You don't want my help?"

"I didn't say that. I just—why are you here?"

"You mean, why am I just now showing up when you've been in trouble every day of your life since I saw you last? You were—what? —ten?"

I nodded.

"Because this is a turning point, *nena*. Things are not what they seem. You don't have enough information to navigate without grounding your ship on the rocks."

"You just happen to know that?" I asked. "Are you watching me? Is that how you know?"

"Michael," she said.

"Michael. Sure." For someone who wasn't supposed to be helping, he sure found ways to insert himself into the situation.

"I know. He's an asshole. But he's our asshole. Never lose sight of that." Dream pushed past me, marching for the basement stairs.

I jogged at her heels. "Tell me what's wrong."

"That man in your basement?"

"Neutralized," I said.

She shook her head. "No. He's a contagion."

I'd left him down there with the rest of my family. With my daughter.

Most of them had already been infected once by the soul sickness of the Horseman Pestilence. They'd come close to dying. That couldn't happen again.

"You misunderstand." Dream yanked open the basement door, the light from the naked bulb on the landing lighting her face like an angel's. She yelled down the steps. "Miguel!"

Beth crowded behind me. "As if anyone down there heard that."

The protections muffled sounds, sometimes a lot, sometimes entirely—for us.

Miguel's voice echoed up the stairwell. "Holy shit. You're here? You can't be here."

Apparently, Michael wasn't the only one who could circumvent magical protections.

I followed Dream down. Miguel met us at the bottom, and Dream enveloped him in her arms as she'd done to me.

"Where is he?" she asked.

He didn't bother to ask how she knew about Mark or what the problem was. There was obviously a problem, and that was good enough. "He's with Addie. She's debriefing him. Then we're gonna let him go."

Dream's head bobbed in a curt nod. She stepped around Miguel and through the magical veil, into the basement's chill. Her sneakers squeaked on the concrete.

Mark had moved from the chair to one of the floor pillows. Addie sat beside him, listening without interrupting as he spoke. Sunday had kept her post by the side door. The kids, including Faith, had moved into Miguel's position when he answered Dream's call.

I checked body language and halos. I listened for lies in every way I knew how. I heard nothing unexpected. There was no danger here that I could sense.

But *mi abuelita* believed differently.

At her station by the side door, Sunday stared. "Is that—"

I nodded.

The kids studied Dream as if she were a threat. I couldn't blame them. The last Elder that had dropped by unannounced and uninvited had tried to kill us all.

Addie turned her attention to Dream as if she'd expected the Elder. "Why are you here?"

Dream pointed at Mark. "You—you're just a baby. No knowledge of what you're capable of—or what you carry. Come here."

Mark looked at Addie for confirmation.

Addie shrugged.

Mark swallowed hard. "You're not like the rest of them, are you?"

"No. I'm scarier. Mind me. Give me your hand."

He did as she asked.

She held up his palm, studying the curves and edges, tracing the lines in his skin with a fingertip.

"Do you know your destiny?" she asked.

"No one does."

"You show others their tender places because yours are so plain to see."

He shook his head. "What does that even mean?"

"You show them what they don't want to see or know about themselves, and they hate you for it."

"Sounds like a curse," he said.

"Sometimes it is. But it can also be a blessing," she countered. "Don't be afraid."

"Usually when people tell me there's nothing to fear, I start looking for the bogeyman."

"You're a smart man," she said.

He pressed his lips into a thin line. "I thought I was a baby?"

She waved him off. "Addie, help me get him up."

Addie set her hands on her hips. "What for?"

"You're really going to ask my reasons? Threads within threads. Webs within webs. Every action changes the warp and weft of all the worlds. We'll be here all day talking about what for and why, and we don't have all day."

Addie held Dream's gaze a moment, then offered her hand to Mark.

Dream hauled him upright with so much strength and speed, it spun him. He held onto her arm to get his bearings.

"I want to go home," he said. "If it's safe to go."

"You're safe," she said. "Don't worry. Just one more thing for you to do here."

She led him out of the inner circle, toward the edge of the second. Toward me.

Red leaned forward from where he stood behind me and spoke low in my ear. "I don't like this. They come to you in dreams unless you summon them. They don't show up in flesh and blood."

But they had lately. Before, the stakes had always been high—crazy high. The Elders had never fought beside me or put in an appearance when I was on the edge of death or helped heal my soul-sick friends.

Dream slowed to a stop in front of me with Mark in tow. She took his hand and reached for me. The movement was so sudden—so unexpected—and with Red and Beth standing directly behind me, I couldn't move.

CHAPTER 8

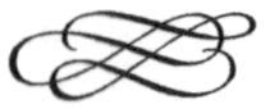

DON'T LET HIM TOUCH YOU.

Those were Michael's words, shouted inside my mind when we'd confronted Mark outside. When the guy had still been possessed by the End. Infected with the End's—what had Dream called it?—contagion.

The temperature in the basement seemed to drop ten degrees. The fine hairs on my arms stood at attention. My magic twined with the Angel's. We aimed for Dream, slicing through her moon-over-the-water halo, through the patch of brown skin between her dark eyes, and into her mind.

We reached for the roots of her thoughts, for the animal instinctual hindbrain that allowed her to move and speak. Everything we touched, everything around which we closed the fist of our magic to hold on, to exert control—vanished as if it were made of vapor and wishes.

Dreams.

My heart raced. I pulled on the link I shared with Red, broadcasting the threat. I breathed in a burst of grass and earth as he began to move. A fraction of a second later, I started to fall back. Too late.

Mark's hand, spooned inside Dream's, brushed my cheek and came to rest there. Just for a moment.

Mark no longer held a piece of the End within him. He was no longer dangerous. I'd staked my life and the lives of my people on that. We'd taken every precaution. We'd made sure it was safe.

Safety was an illusion.

Dream let go of his hand. "Night, Red, Beth—will you step out of the way and let him pass? He wants to go home, like he said."

Beth did as Dream asked. Neither Red nor I moved an inch, but Beth's sidestep gave Mark enough room to squirm past us and take off. He slid through the veil and out of sight and hearing.

I looked at Dream, locking my gaze on hers. "What the hell just happened?"

"You needed that," she said.

"That what?"

"The push."

Red shook his head. "There's no magic left in him. No ill will in his heart."

"Honey, one day you're going to learn that heart isn't everything, that love isn't always enough, and that humans are not as good as you'd like to believe."

He beetled his brows.

"It's not that complicated." She turned from him to look at me, sadness filling her eyes. "You're angry. You have a right to be, *nena*."

My heart was a tangle of feelings. Love. Confusion. Betrayal. Anger rode on top of them all.

The kids moved as one unit from their place by the laundry to form a physical and magical barrier behind Dream. Jess and her night sky full of stars. Ben and his stone shield. Corey, with her bone-white halo that marked her as a speaker to and for the dead. Faith, her silver-and-gold halo brassy and sharp-edged.

Dream didn't spare them a single glance. "I'm not going to apologize. I did what needed to be done."

Red filled the space beside me, folding his arms across his chest. "Stop speaking in riddles."

She flashed a rueful smile. "The archangel is a puppet master here. He says, 'Oh, I can't help you. You'll have to do this without me.' And then he slips inside your head and compels you to do his bidding and you go right along with it, *nena.* Right along with it without so much as a question. Didn't I raise you better?"

"I have few memories of you," I said.

"But they're strong. Think for yourself. Do what I instilled in you."

"The Order raised me," I said.

She waved the statement way as if it weren't worthy of comment. As if the Order's influence on me counted for nothing—or next to nothing.

"When you're boxed in and left with nothing but terrible choices, you find a way through that no one else would be able to find. You always find it," she said.

Sunday started toward us from her place at the side door, her rose-red halo burning like a fire, her voice growing louder with every word. "You're right. She does. She's been hunted. Her soul has disintegrated twice and been rebuilt, first by her victims and then by the Angel of fucking Death. She's almost died physically too many times to count and now she's turning into Death—what else could the wings and the shifts in her magic mean?—and that's not enough for you. You had to come along and do something else to her. What did you do?"

Dream met her gaze. "I got her to let her guard down."

Sunday stepped into her personal space, closing until they were nose to nose. "Dirty tricks, *abuelita.* What about the magic you helped the infected normal pass to her?"

Michael's warning had been specific. As had his words when I'd first seen him on the street.

"The people the End infected or possessed—whatever you want to call it—Michael called them signs of the Apocalypse," I said. "My guess is that they're all like Mark. Normal. No special reason to be chosen. Other than proximity to me."

"I have proximity to you," Sunday said.

Faith shook her head. "You can defend yourself, Aunt Sunday. You're close enough that I'd notice right away if you weren't acting like yourself. We all would. We'd know something was wrong. Same with the rest of us. Some of us are closer to each other and some not, but we're all connected. We've shared our most private thoughts and our magic. We're not impossible to make a move on, but why risk it when there are plenty of people out on the street, going about their business, who have no knowledge or defenses against your magic? Who none of us would suspect of being dangerous?"

"Faith's right," Red said.

Sunday nodded reluctantly. "I know. But that still doesn't answer the question I put to Night's grandmother."

I swallowed hard. "Michael also said that I was a sign. Is Mark's magic part of that?"

Dream nodded. "It's what turns you, finally."

"Turns me into what?"

"*La Muerte.*"

I stared at her, pretending for the moment not to hear the sound that Faith had swallowed, something between a keen and a whimper.

Beth pushed forward, placing herself between Dream and me. "I thought you were her friend."

Dream looked at Beth as if she were an insect. "What would you know about friendship? You have no friends in this world or any other. No one who truly loves you except the serpent. And now you've messed that up by disobeying orders."

Beth narrowed her eyes. "World-class deflection."

Dream cocked her head, chin raised. "I'm not her friend. I've never been. I'm a guide."

"You're a person with an agenda," Beth said. "Which makes you no different than the rest of them. Why's it so important to you that Night becomes the big reaper?"

"It's what she was born for," Dream said. "She stands on the shoulders of her ancestors, every one of whom worked their asses off to get her to this point, to fulfill her destiny."

"What about what Night wants?"

"What Night wants doesn't matter."

I begged to differ.

"She was genetically engineered to become Death? How do you do that? I'm curious."

"Curiosity kills," Dream said.

"I know," Beth said matter-of-factly. "So, not genetically engineered. Magically engineered?"

Dream held her gaze and said nothing, which was as good as saying yes.

"Don't say her destiny is 'to bring about the Apocalypse,' because that would not be cool."

Dream shook her head. "To stop it. The Angel of Death is the only being with enough power to prevent the end of all things."

My breath seemed to seize in my lungs. I shuddered at my core, the vibration moving from inside to the surface of my skin.

I'd known what was happening even before Beth first brought it up the first time—that I would change. That the Angel and I would become a sum greater than our parts. I'd feared the thought of it, even as the reality set in. Every time the Angel and I joined our magic, we drew closer. The shape of my magic had changed to reflect his, and, if I wasn't mistaken, for his to reflect mine. The wings that cradled and protected my heart, that moved as a sign that something of significance was happening, that I should pay attention, were one thing. The wings that had grown on the outside were something else.

Could I reverse what had happened? If I tried to, what would that mean for me? For the Angel?

I'd had no time to consider those questions. Things were moving too fast. Enemies on all sides. Barely time to deal with each new situation and catch my breath. No time to look at the big picture.

"What does that mean for me?" I asked.

Dream took her time answering. "It's not about you."

Beth nodded. "You're the sacrifice, Night. You don't matter here except to play a role."

Dream glared at her.

"Tell me I'm wrong," Beth said.

Dream opened her mouth to speak, then snapped it shut. She could do no such thing.

"The memories I have of you—they're all lies," I said. "You pretended to love me, to be the one person who never judged me, who was never afraid of me, who helped me understood who I was."

"They're not lies," Dream said. "I meant all of it."

"But it wasn't personal. You didn't love *me*, you loved what I might become."

She closed her eyes a moment. When she opened them again, I could see the light of the moon reflected in their depths. "You make it sound so simple."

"I was a little girl who would never have survived without your love. It is that simple."

"You're not a little girl anymore," she said.

No, I wasn't. "What happens now?"

"You become. You do what you do, and we see what happens."

"No marching orders?" Beth asked.

Dream answered Beth's question, but she had eyes only for me. "Unlike Michael, I understand the futility of telling my granddaughter what to do."

"But you would if you could," Beth said.

"No," she said to me, and the sound of that word falling from her lips was like a door closing—forever. "Unlike the others, I trust you, *nena.*"

I didn't believe her. I didn't believe anything about her anymore.

Sorrow seemed to rise from her heart, filling her face like water lifted by a tide. In the space of a breath, the boundaries of her body became indistinct. Her flesh and blood and bones faded, as if she'd never been there at all. As if she'd been only imagined, and not real. In her place, only a puddle of water remained. A skim of water on the concrete, a reflection of the moon moving within it.

I stared at the moon, and it stared back at me. It said nothing, but it didn't have to. Its language was betrayal.

Sunday blinked. "The fuck?"

"She left in style. Her work here was done," Beth said. "No need to hang around and catch the epilogue."

Miguel moved from his place near the foot of the stairs, passing through the veil of protections without a sound.

Faith shouted after him. "Where are you going?"

And when he didn't answer, she turned the question on me. "Where's he going? Mom, what's happening? I'm scared."

I looked at her, but I didn't know how to answer.

After that, the voices no longer sounded like those of my friends, only waves of sound roiling and crashing against a distant shore. The roar of them filled my head until there was no place for my own thoughts. The air no longer chilled my skin, it scalded—not heat, but ice. My vision began to blur.

I shook my head to clear it, but the motion only shook up the fragments of sound and feeling, shattering them into shards of color and light that rained down behind my eyes. The wings that surrounded my heart squeezed until I gasped for breath and my legs gave out. I hit the floor on my knees, breaking the surface of the water, chasing the moon away.

Voices rose around me. I couldn't make sense of them. I couldn't understand. The hell was happening to me?

Two words cut through to my core. They tasted of grass and earth.

"Everyone, stop talking."

Words. Not directed at me.

The thrash of sound ceased.

"Follow Miguel. Check the perimeter and make sure we're locked down good and tight," Red said.

I held tight to the shape of his words. To the colors in his voice. Soft green. Dark, rich brown.

"What's wrong with her?" my daughter asked. Her words trembled in the air, the color of her twinned halo. Silver and gold.

My daughter.

"I don't know, Faith."

"Not good enough. Something's wrong. Something bad."

"She'll be all right," he said. It sounded like a prayer.

"Where are you taking her?"

"Upstairs."

"And then what?"

Sunday pushed her way into the fray. "One of us needs to go after Mark. He's dangerous to us and everyone else out there."

"No," Red said. "No one leaves this house. I don't care what kind of badass you are, it's not happening."

"Don't tell me—"

"We can't afford to lose you," he said. "Any of you."

I didn't hear her answer.

The shards of color and light began to cut me, slicing into my mind. Into my magic. My vision grayed and faded until only a single point of light remained. Then that, too, fled like a terrified animal, leaving me alone in the dark.

CHAPTER 9

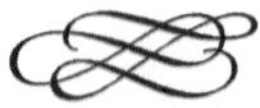

I CAME TO in the dark. For a long moment, I thought I was dreaming or hallucinating. I couldn't make out any shapes or sounds. Fear gripped my heart in its angry fist. Then the house sighed around me as if it'd been holding its breath, and that sigh was relief.

Gradually, my vision picked up gradations of light and shadow. Wan moonlight filtering through the edges of the covered window. The round back of the chair in the corner and the clothes strewn across its arms and seat. The square shape of the night table and the half-full glass of water balanced on top. Beside it, my knife, the silver glint of the blade in the spare light a warning.

Then I began to feel, sensations making themselves known for what they were and what they meant. The rise and fall of Red's chest against my back. Steady breathing, but not deep enough to signal sleep. His arm around my waist. His knees tucked behind mine. The strong scent of his magic. Love.

"It's okay," he said. "You're okay."

I tried to call him a liar, because how could that possibly be true? But my voice felt rusty, as if I hadn't used it in a long time. I cleared my throat, and different words flowed instead. "How long have I been out?"

"About twenty-four hours."

An entire day. While the world turned outside and the End and Famine continued to move the world closer to destruction. While my family worried that I might not wake up. And, if and when I did, would I be the same?

"Mark?" I asked.

"No idea. Got bigger fish to fry."

"Is everyone else all right?" I asked. "Did Sunday do what you asked?"

"She's still here," he said. "We're okay. Faith is okay. The enemy's left us alone."

No reason for them to do that. We were vulnerable. They should've attacked already. They should be attacking now. Unless—

"They're waiting for something."

"Must be," he said.

And I was laid up in here. I tried to push up on my elbow. *Tried.* My arm felt weak, as if the muscles had forgotten how to work. They felt hot inside the skin, too, as if they had a fever.

"Sunday—"

"—and Miguel have our security in hand. They're working with Addie and the house spirit and Beth to do what needs to be done. Relax."

"You're kidding."

"You're sick, Night."

"I don't think so. Not in the traditional way."

He didn't say anything. He didn't have to.

I reached for *La Muerte* with my mind, expecting to hear the Angel's voice in my head, expecting to feel the flutter of wings around my heart. Neither of those things occurred.

I took a deep breath and held it, a shudder running through my body from the soles of my feet to the crown of my head. I remembered everything that had happened precisely until the moment Mark had touched my cheek. From there, my memories felt more like shattered glass, painted with colors and faces and words, spun in the wheel of a kaleidoscope like the one my father had given me when I was five.

My grandmother betrayed me, told me she trusted me, and then drifted apart like a fever dream on waking. All that was left of her became the moon's reflection on a still pool of water that hugged the basement floor.

She'd left me. She'd done something to me in the collision with Mark. She'd set something in motion that could not now be stopped. The Angel and I would become a sign of the apocalypse.

"I've got that part. I mean what happened after she left?"

"You lost consciousness. You were there…and not. Your body faded in and out. I saw the Angel inside of you, Night, pressed up against the edges of your skin. It looked like he was trying to get free. It was like something from a horror movie."

I didn't recall any of that. If Faith had seen that? A splinter of fear speared my heart. "Did the others—?"

"Just me and Addie. We didn't say anything. We didn't want to freak anyone out more than they already were."

"What do you see now?"

He hesitated.

"Tell me."

"It's progressing. The Angel is becoming more solid. More…"

"More what?"

"Real."

"More real than me. Is that what you're trying to say?"

"It's what I don't want to say."

I rolled over to face him. It took a long, excruciating minute to maneuver until I could see his face. Sweat beaded on my forehead and the nape of my neck, warm at first but turning cold as I caught a glimpse of the lines etched across his forehead and the pressed, straight line of his mouth.

He cradled my face in his hands, words spilling out in a flow that escalated from careful to a barely controlled rush. "I never thought— you've been changing ever since you trapped the Angel inside your head, Night. It seems like it was always headed this way. I ignored it as best I could until the wings started to grow out of your back. They made it real. They were the ticking clock. And now, with what your grandmother started, the change is accelerating. And it's not just your magic that's shifting—it's the Angel's. It's happening so fast, I don't know how you made it through the night. I don't know whether you'll make it through the next."

I took a deep breath and blew it out slowly. "I'll fight it."

"You have been," he said. "I can see your every cell fighting. The magic in your body refusing to cede control. That's the only reason you're still you at all."

The truth in his words hit me like a fist to the gut. "You're saying I'm losing the battle."

"Can't you feel it?"

I didn't want to feel it. I didn't want to look closely enough. "I don't know."

"Yes, you do."

I shook my head. I didn't want to understand just how far gone I might be.

"I'm fucking scared, Night."

Small tremors began at my core, traveling along every nerve. I knew how he felt.

A crash sounded from upstairs, followed by a stream of cuss words bellowed at the top of Addie's lungs.

My voice shook. I tried to steady it and failed. "She trying to bring down the house?"

"She's trying to summon Michael."

She'd done it once before, days—or a million years—ago. "It's not going well, is it?"

Red shook his head. "She figures if anyone can stop this, it's him."

"He's not supposed to help us. It's against the rules." Whatever that meant. Whoever laid down a law strong enough to compel archangels. Damn the consequences.

"He's remarkably selective with his rule-breaking."

I listened for *La Muerte*'s voice inside me once again. I felt for his presence. I still felt nothing. I wondered whether it was because the Angel was me now, and I was him.

"Maybe he can't do anything," I said.

"That's bullshit. Don't give him an easy out."

I wasn't. I still thought he was an asshole. I still hated his archangel guts.

Michael and the End and the games they played, the strategies they used to maneuver—I might never understand it. Dream and what she'd done were way over my head, so far over my head that the hurt in my heart meant nothing against any of their schemes and plans.

"Maybe he's done everything he could already," I said.

Red closed his eyes against the thought. Words he couldn't say. Words he didn't want to hear. When he opened them again, they were filled with unshed tears.

"What do we do, Night?"

If Michael couldn't be reached and I couldn't talk with the Angel— then all that was left were the moments I had and the people I loved.

"Kiss me," I said.

He rolled closer, resting his forehead against mine. He held my gaze for a heartbeat before his lips brushed mine, the grass and earth of his magic rising to meet the icy night sky within me. He deepened the kiss, gentle with love and rough with fear. The heart link between us filled with the bright and dark of it all. With who we were right now, in this moment.

I memorized the feel of him, the taste of him—I knew those things like I knew my own patchwork soul, but now with everything in me shifting and changing, who knew what would emerge? How much would I still recall? Would Red still be a part of me?

I didn't want him to pull away when he did. I fisted his shirt in my hands, holding on as tightly as I could, and swallowed hard. I'd do everything I could to stay with them, right up until the last free breath I took. I'd help them survive even if the person recognizable as me did not. I'd do whatever I could until I had no control. Until my heart stopped beating.

"Help me up, Red."

"You can't even sit. You want to walk?"

"I don't care what it takes," I said.

"What are you gonna do?"

I met his gaze. He took one look at my eyes and eased me up to sit. It hurt to be upright—the pressure of my weight, the air on my skin, the rawness in my muscles. I breathed through it. I drew my magic front and center, calling it into service—not against someone else, but for myself.

I closed my eyes, relief rushing through me as my view of the world outside my mind dimmed and the strain of taking in pulses and waves of light and life force eased. When even seeing felt overwhelming, how could I do what needed to be done?

My magic obeyed my will. I still had that.

I sent it into my own mind, into my memories. Not the kind I usually slipped inside. Not memories of the heart, but body memories. Muscle memories.

How did it feel to be strong? How did it feel to have so much life force coursing through me that I burned with it, that I shone with it, that it overflowed my skin and met the life force of the world? When the act of breathing felt like a kiss. When curling my fingers into a fist felt like the heart of power.

Those memories gathered around me like fireflies on a balmy summer night, a thousand lights in the darkness. They settled on my skin, each flutter of wings a caress.

The wings around my heart stirred. The Angel, responding.

I waited a beat for more, but *La Muerte* was silent and still.

On one long, deep breath, the firefly memories sank into my skin, into muscle and blood and bone. On a second, they settled there, masking my screaming nerves. One moment, the pain was there. The next, it was gone.

On the third breath, the tension fled my body. The pain of holding myself up drained away. I opened my eyes again, taking in the light and magic of the room around me, drawing in the glorious scent and flavor of Red's magic.

He slid a finger beneath my chin and turned my head an inch, running his gaze over every inch of my face. "What did you do?"

"What I had to."

He raised his hand to cup the side of my face. "How long will the magic last?"

"Until the well of my magic runs dry—"

"Until you have nothing left to give."

I nodded.

"How long is that?"

"I don't know. Like you said, everything's changing so fast. I've bought a little time, I think."

He opened his mouth to tell me differently.

I raised a hand to stop him. "All of my life, I've only used my magic in short bursts. I trap the target. I kill the target. Maybe, if I need to, I hold them—but not for long. This is something different. I don't know how deep or how full my well of magic actually is. Maybe it's more than I think because of the Angel—"

"Or maybe it's less, and what you're doing now will burn you out faster. Maybe it'll accelerate your transformation."

"We'll find out," I said.

"Did you hear me when I told you I was scared?"

"Loud and clear. I don't think we have any not-scary options right now."

He didn't want to accept that. The struggle was written all over his face.

"You're not the only one who's afraid here, Red."

He swallowed hard. "I didn't mean—"

"I know." I considered my words, but they refused to fit into the neat, non-alarming boxes I tried to jam them into. "Who is the Angel of Death, Red? What is he? If I think I know because we've shared the same flesh-and-blood housing for the last few months, I'm fooling myself. He's enormous. He's so big and so old that I can't even wrap my head around it.

"I haven't had the chance to figure it out yet, if I could even begin to. We've been running from one crisis to another. From one near-death situation to another. Just trying to stay one step ahead."

"Trying to stay alive," he said.

I rolled over whatever he planned to say next. "I don't know who the Angel is, but I'm on my way to finding out. What happens when there's no difference at all between who I am and who he is? I'm terrified that I'll lose myself. That I'll be someone else. Someone unrecognizable."

I took deep breaths—one, two, three. I could barely get enough air, and I needed more before I could go on. Four, five, six.

"I lost myself before—you know that," I said. "I had no soul left. I was dead inside, Red. And now I have this life. This crazy, unbelievable life that I've worked so hard for against all odds, and I know how fortunate I am. I have you. I have Faith. Sunday. God, even Addie. I have a family now. I can't give all that away. I can't. You're talking about surviving? I won't survive that, Red. Not the important parts of me. Whatever ethical compass I have will die along with my humanity."

I felt winded, as if I'd taken a long run uphill at a distance beyond my endurance. The whole thing felt like more than I could endure.

He swallowed every word as if they were stones. He held all of their weight. He straddled my legs so that he could look at me head-on, resting his hands on my shoulders.

"You'll choose right," he said.

"You can't be sure of that."

"Yes, I can. I trust you, Night."

"That's what she said."

"Your grandmother? Fuck Dream. I'm not her. I'm human." He reached for my hand and pressed it to his chest. "You feel that?"

The beating of his heart. Strong. Sure.

I tried to pull my hand back. He refused to let it go.

"Hear what I'm saying, Night."

"You trust me. Maybe you shouldn't—not anymore."

He nodded. "I'm not her. I'm not a power with an agenda. I'm yours. I know you'll choose right because I know you. I love you. And because if I see you falling, I'll pick you back up."

I took another deep breath and blew it out slowly. They were words, no matter whose. They shouldn't make me feel better in the face of what was coming, but they did. "I'll hold you to that."

"You'd better."

"That's the right answer," I said.

He lifted my hand to his lips and kissed my fingertips. Only then did he let go. "So, what now?"

"Now, we fight."

"Who? What?"

"You really think Famine and the End have retreated? Because I don't."

He shook his head. "They're still out there, planning something worse than last time."

"Not for long."

He climbed off of me, reaching to help me up. I took his hand, settling on my own two feet as if nothing was wrong.

"How do you feel?" he asked.

I still felt no pain, even though somewhere deep inside, my muscles and nerves screamed. I had no issues with balance, even though I knew without a doubt that, without the magic I'd used on myself, I'd have fallen.

"Okay for now." Now was what mattered.

"I'll catch up," he said.

I raised a brow.

"I have something I need to do here."

Something he wanted to handle by himself.

"Don't worry."

I nodded.

He opened the bedroom door for me. I slipped out of our quiet sanctuary to sound and fury and the mouth-watering perfume of pot roast. I was going to battle for my family, to save them or die trying.

Down the hall in the front room, I found my family preparing for war. They were going to battle for me. For all of us.

Afternoon sun leaked through the edges and imperfections of the drawn window blinds in the living room and the kitchen, scattering long, thin spears of light across the hardwood like children's toys. The walls glowed with magic so strong, I could've used a pair of sunglasses to look at it without feeling blinded by its power.

The house spirit, beefed up beyond its everyday level, courtesy of Addie. A layer of stone-gray shielding, carefully placed by Ben. Traps laid into the shield that bore both a Watcher's signature and Jess's distinct flavor, traps meant to reweave the reality around the unwary soul who triggered them—in other words, to transport them somewhere else.

At every door and window, a writhing orange-and-black serpent circled the frame. Beth had used her blood to create them, spelling them to poison. Her poison, like her boss's, killed.

Ben and Jess placed weapons strategically around the living and dining rooms—kitchen knives, mostly, but also fireplace pokers and a baseball bat. Corey sat cross-legged in the center, her white halo shining and head bowed. I couldn't see her face behind the fall of her red hair, but I heard the whisper of her voice and the power in it as she called on the dead to protect us.

Sunday ducked her head through the kitchen door. "It's under control."

"The front of the house," I said. "What about out back?"

"Double the protections. Double the fun." Her mouth quirked into a grin. She didn't look worried, but she had the edge about her that meant an oncoming fight. Every second she held my gaze, it grew sharper.

"Where's Faith?" I asked.

"In your room now," she said. "Extending the protections, closing up the holes, making sure everything is one hundred percent. Don't worry."

"Second time in five minutes someone's told me not to worry."

"You should listen to us."

"I am. What aren't you telling me?"

"You look like shit."

"Thanks."

"I was trying to keep that to myself, but I thought you should know."

I held her gaze.

She rolled her eyes. "Fine. Addie's making you a sandwich. Don't ask her about Michael. Or ask her if you want."

"He didn't come."

"He didn't come," she said.

No surprise there.

The surprise was that I didn't feel hungry in spite of having been out for so long. In spite of the amount of energy I'd used to effect the magic that allowed me to stand and move. "I don't want a sandwich."

Addie raised her voice to carry. "You'll eat what I put in front of you, Night Sanchez."

I didn't need to see the willful expression on her face to know that her lips would be pursed and her stare would be firm and disapproving. I heard all of that in her voice just fine.

I stepped past Sunday, into the heart of Addie's home, my feet familiar with the paths worn on the tile, and settled into the chair Addie had pulled out for me. I ran my fingertips along the marred edge of the oak table, my memory familiar with the splintered spots and circles left by cold, wet glasses and extra hot plates. The stuff of life.

How long would I care about those things? How long would I recall them?

I shook my head to clear it.

Addie, her Milky Way halo filled with exploding stars so bright they set her face aglow, placed a plate down in front of me. The promised sandwich—roast beef, of course—a pile of greasy salt-and-vinegar chips, and a pickle. She poured me the last cup of coffee from the pot on the counter—more sludge than joe—and set that down with enough force to splash some of the contents over the rim, splattering the sleeve of her purple dress.

"Is that mad for me?" I asked. "I know it's not at me."

She shook her head. "Oh, yes it is. I know what you did to yourself in there and I want to tell you that you shouldn't have, that it will only make things worse, that when your strength runs out, you'll be as vulnerable as a goddamn baby and I'm afraid none of us will be able to help you then. You understand?"

"What else was I supposed to do?"

Addie sighed. "Nothing. I don't know."

Sunday dropped into the chair beside me, bracing her booted foot against the edge of the table. Shoes on in the house had become a thing. Too many threats, too fast. But shoes on the kitchen table were designed to set Addie off.

Addie's tone hardened. "Miss. Sloan."

"We're beyond the end of the world now, Addie. I don't think my foot on the table matters that much anymore."

"You're disrespecting my home. Disrespecting me. I won't have it."

"Make me stop."

Addie stared at her.

"Do more than seethe and say a few words. You're too angry. You're spoiling for a fight, but you're holding it all in—or most of it. Too much of it."

Addie blinked. "You're *managing* me?"

"You're going to explode at the worst possible moment, and we don't need that," Sunday said.

Addie took her time replying. "You realize I could unmake you? I could erase you from this earth?"

Sunday shrugged.

"You have a death wish."

"You're not the first person to say so."

Addie nodded slowly. "I take your point. Now get your mother-fucking foot off my table."

Sunday obliged. Slowly.

"What were we talking about?" Addie asked.

"Losing Night as we know her forever after she goes full-on Angel of Death."

"Night as you know her," Addie said. "Not we."

Sunday's turn to stare.

"I only met you a few months ago, Night. Wasn't a full twenty-four hours before you ended up with the Angel in you."

"You worried about what I'll do?" I asked.

"Yes," she said.

"No beating around the bush. I appreciate that."

"I'll make sure the others are safe no matter what happens. You can count on that."

"Good." I pushed away from the table and picked up my sandwich, forcing myself to take a bite before I stood up. Still no issue physically. That was good, too.

I had a job to do. I needed to get to it.

The flavors of roast beef and—a gift, avocado—came alive in my mouth. I was hungry enough after all, and made short work of the sandwich on my way down the hall, checking every wall and window in every room, making sure that the protections were strong and true.

I figured I'd catch Faith in Red's and my room, but she'd already gone. The magical shields she'd built were flawless. She'd done as good a job as any Order operative. That thought made me feel alternately proud and sick inside. The things my kid had grown up with— always looking over her shoulder.

It was a trauma, like what had happened to Mark all his life. Like what had happened to all of us at one time or another. None of us had escaped life unscathed.

There was more of that on the horizon. I understood all of that in my head. My heart was another story.

I forced my feet to move, one in front of the other. I had to check the rest of the house. I needed eyes on everything if I was going to be effective. If I was going to protect anyone at all against what was coming.

I found Faith with Red in the last room, the one where the kids slept—even Jess, who had her own bedroom upstairs. They wanted to stay together. They were stronger together.

Red and Faith sat across from each other on air mattresses strewn with unmade flannel sheets and dirty socks, reminiscent of the room the kids had made for themselves in the hideout they'd squatted in a couple of months ago. They'd been afraid the Angel and I would hurt Faith. They'd created a safe space.

There it was again, that word. Safe.

I shook it off.

In spite of the fact that the majority of the room's residents were girls of the femme variety, the space stank of dirty socks—Ben's. Too bad I couldn't open a window without opening an obvious hole in our protections.

Faith had tucked her long fall of dark hair into a braid that skimmed the middle of her back. Her brown eyes looked huge, as if they were trying to take in everything she saw, as if she were trying to remember every detail. Worry lines furrowed her brow. My hourglass pendant hung around her neck as always.

At the sight of me, she wrapped her hand around it, holding it tightly. "Hey, Mom."

She'd called me that fewer than ten times in all the years we'd been together. I studied her, looking for shifts in her silver-and-gold halo, catching a glimpse of tarnished concern, a dull gleam of fear, and a fiery refusal to allow that fear its head.

Red glanced at me from the corner of his eye, trying not to be obvious about reading me. If he saw anything markedly different than he had twenty minutes ago, he showed no sign. He moved over to make room for me.

"I can't stay," I said. "But I'll be right back. Just need to check the backyard."

Faith rose. "I'll come with you. I need to see what you see."

I started to tell her no, that she should stay with Red, but the words died on my tongue. The days when she didn't need to understand our strategy because she was too young or couldn't defend herself or didn't have the power to go on the offensive were past.

"Come on," I said.

I gestured for her to walk ahead of me, glancing over my shoulder at Red as she stepped out the door, asking my question with a raised brow. *Coming?*

He shook his head. "Spend time with her."

Better now than later. Better now, while I still could.

I followed Faith out and glided past her, circling back around to the kitchen and the back door, nodding at Sunday and Addie, who huddled at the table, talking in hushed tones. Faith's and my coats were draped over the back of the chair closest to the door. I knew Sunday had fetched them from the front room. I didn't need her to throw me a reassuring glance or curve her lips into a tight smile to know it'd been her, but I appreciated those things all the same.

She knew me so well. Knew that I'd want to check out back, that I'd need some air.

I slipped into my coat. Faith followed suit.

Stepping through the back door was like walking through gelatin, only without the sticky residue. The beefed-up shields recognized us. If they hadn't, that thick, viscous layer between inside and outside would've tried to kill us. I took some comfort in that.

The shoveled porch was occupied. Beth's orange halo writhed more than usual, its black snakes agitated and aching to strike. She'd gathered her mess of braids with a rubber band from Addie's kitchen drawer. She cradled a mug of fresh coffee in both hands, her body relaxed, but the sharp gaze behind her black-framed glasses caught and analyzed every detail of the oncoming night.

"Anything?" I asked.

She shook her head. "Not yet."

Shadows crouched beneath the towering fir trees to our left. The snow had melted from their branches, but still skirted their trunks. The rest of the yard was mostly clear, the grass stunned and silent, the shed sullen at far end. All of it radiated a distinct orange-and-black glow. Outside the chain-link fence on the right, the driveway was clear. No snow. No ice.

"You take care of that?" I asked.

"I thought about not shoveling it. Chances are, the snow and ice that melted in the sun would leave the drive all wet, and when the temp drops again like it's doing, the wet would refreeze. That could be nifty in case of an attack, right? But it's a double-edged sword. Or a double-edged driveway that could come back to bite us in the ass. Anyway, I needed something to do."

"You've done plenty."

"I'm antsy. I'm not used to waiting to be attacked. I'm used to sudden, surgical strikes that I have to defend against or die. And going on the offensive. I like the offensive."

"It won't be much longer," I said.

"How do you know?"

"The longer they wait, the more time they give us to prepare."

Faith cleared her throat. "I don't think so."

I glanced over my shoulder to meet her gaze.

"The longer they wait, the more time they allow for you to become the Angel of Death. They're waiting for that to happen."

Beth cocked her head, considering. "They think the Angel will be on their side?"

"That would be extra," Faith said. "The Angel doesn't give a shit about the rest of us, only about Night, and that's probably because he needs her, not because he likes her. No offense."

I shook my head. "None taken."

The Angel wasn't human. Ascribing human emotions to him was a fool's game.

"The minute the Angel takes over, he's outta here. He's got stuff to do, right? An apocalypse to—"

"Stop," I said. "He's on the side of life."

"It doesn't matter, Mom. The point is, he'll leave us. We have a lot of firepower, but you're the one who brings us all together. Who strategizes. Who understands what's happening at a level the rest of us can't even comprehend."

She was selling herself and the others short. I opened my mouth to say so, but she held up a hand to stop me.

"Without you, the group falls apart."

"What about Sunday? What about Red? Addie?"

"Hey," Beth said. "Standing right here. Good at strategy. Got connections."

Faith ignored her. "Sunday is a bomb. She points herself at the problem and explodes. She doesn't think the way you do. She doesn't consider that the rest of us are human people with human feelings. We're strong, but we're fragile, too. She's not."

"I think you don't know your Aunt Sunday as well as you believe you do."

She huffed. "Anyway, do you really think Sunday or Red is going to stick around? They go where you go."

I didn't know what to say. I wanted to tell her she was wrong, but I couldn't be sure. So I said nothing. That was better than platitudes or lying.

I scanned the yard again to search for any sign of infiltration, but I needed to avert my gaze just as much. To let the gravity of Faith's words sink in like a stone dropped into deep water, making its shape and weight known only after it sliced through the current and kissed the bottom.

The yard held no sign of Famine or the End. No enemies other than my own miscalculation. My kid had to point out the obvious to me. *Me.* My Order training and experience was more than sufficient for me to have figured that out on my own. Hell, it should've been the first plausible enemy plan I dealt with. Instead, I'd acted as if invasion were the foregone conclusion.

I'd refused to go there because I'd refused to admit I would lose the fight for my humanity.

"What's everyone talking about inside?" I asked.

"The plan to kill you if you turn on us," Beth said matter-of-factly.

Faith stepped alongside me. "What to do without you."

I nodded. I'd blinded myself by refusing to do what was expected of me. I hated being cornered into someone else's plan. Someone else's expectations. I hated feeling like a rat in a trap. Or a winged creature that might fly away at the first goddamn opportunity.

I spoke to the Angel, calling his name, words echoing inside my mind.

I didn't think he'd answer. He hadn't said a thing since the change had begun in earnest. Was he biding his time? Had he lost his voice? Was I no longer worth talking with, beneath his notice? Was he as rattled as I was?

A single, solitary feather stirred beside my heart.

I held my breath.

CHAPTER 10

I N THE DEPTHS of my mind, the Angel whispered. I couldn't make out a word, only the maddening, just-out-of-reach murmur of his voice. I reached for it, grasping, shutting out the cold, the fading light and the danger imminent all around us, Faith's and Beth's presence.

For a heartbeat, the whisper rose on a wave of sound, like water breaking against a barrier. Then it was gone, leaving no sign that it had ever been there at all. My mind quieted. The feather that had stirred beside my heart went still and did not move again.

I took a deep breath and blew it out slowly. There had been something there. He had been there. He'd spoken and I hadn't heard a thing.

Was it some fault in me? An effect of the change happening in my body? Had I imagined the barrier between us?

A hand settled on my shoulder, digging a chink in my concentration. Beth's strident words struck that weakness like a sledgehammer. "What's wrong?"

I glanced at her hand. She removed it.

"Sorry, but that was the third frickin' time I asked you. The hell, Night?"

"I was listening."

"To what?"

Faith looked me up and down. "To him."

"The Angel?" Beth asked.

Faith kept her eyes on me. "He's getting stronger and you're getting weaker. You're getting stronger and he's getting weaker. You're like static between radio stations, not settled one way or the other."

"You can see that?" I asked.

"Red told me."

I nodded. He would've said just that, in plain language, unadorned with nuance. Brass tacks were what they were.

"I'm afraid, Mom." Tears welled, but she looked skyward, refusing to let them fall.

After a moment, she wiped at her eyes with the back of her hand and stalked into the house, slamming the door behind her.

Beth studied her coffee. "So, what now?"

"You're not afraid, too? Everyone is."

From her expression, it was clear she knew I was talking about myself, too. She took her time answering. "Shit happens and the best you can do is deal and pray you come out the other side. I've seen things. Been through things."

Because of her own curiosity and bad judgment—learning the hard way. And then because of Malek. "You still worried about your boss?"

"Why do you want to know?" she asked. "What does it have to do with what's happening here?"

"Is your mind on him or in the game with us?" It came out harsher than I'd meant for it to, but I needed to know.

She raised both brows and tilted her head, ceding the point. "I'm here. Besides, I figure if he was going to kill me, he'd have shown up here to do it already."

About that. "I don't want him here."

"His agenda and yours are the same. On the side of life."

"The way he goes about it is fucked up."

"No argument," she said. "But we might need him."

"We'll cross that bridge—"

She finished my thought. "When we come to it."

I scanned the yard again, marking the changes the last few minutes had wrought. The growing shadows. The chilling air. The silence, marred only by the caw of a single crow as it winged overhead. I stared at it until it flew out of sight.

"Message from Kevin?" Beth asked.

I shook my head.

I appreciated the Faery King's ability to send corvid messengers. They came in handy. I don't know what any of them would have to tell me now.

Our problem was ours to solve. We needed everyone, working together. Faith was right about that.

"Where are Miguel and Stacy?" I asked.

She looked at me from the corner of her eye. "They went out."

"Out where?"

"To the gym," she said. "To secure an escape route in case we need one, and I think we're definitely going to need one. I'm pretty sure we're not all going to get through this one alive and we need to be able to send the most fragile of us—to use Faith's word—out of the line of fire when it gets hairy around here."

"That Faith's idea?"

"Sunday's."

"Anything else I should know?"

Beth nodded at the nearest tree. At the crow perched on edge of its lowest branch. Was it the same crow that had flown over a moment ago? No, it hadn't come back—I felt sure of it.

It focused its gaze on Beth, obviously communicating. I couldn't ask Beth what it said, not out here in the open. I asked her a different question instead.

"What do you think? How long will Famine and the End wait before they come at us?"

Beth blinked. "You're asking for my opinion? I'm not an operative."

I shrugged.

"Seriously, Night. I talk a good game, but I make it by the skin of my teeth."

"You always come through."

She took in the compliment at face value, neither denying nor preening. "I can't give you an answer about the End, but I know Famine. On her own, she doesn't have the patience to wait much longer and she's not a team player. What are you thinking?"

"That I want to go inside. You should come."

She opened the back door and slipped through. I followed, giving the yard one last glance. I felt eyes on me, noting my every small movement, and felt the familiar chiming inside that signaled the presence of another Horseman.

I turned my gaze to the source of the feeling—the shadow growing now on the far side of the shed. Famine was back there. It had to be her, watching and waiting, and for what? Why get close enough to raise my awareness?

She seemed to answer my thought by stepping into the fading daylight, letting me get a look at her. Brown pigtails and black saucer eyes behind tortoiseshell glasses. Navy blue dress. Navy Mary Janes on her feet. She stood with her hands fisted at her sides, muscle corded in her arms from the tension she held.

She opened her mouth to say something, then snapped it shut. The look on her face was pure hatred, but even the single fiery emotion wasn't a simple thing.

This wasn't a good-versus-evil thing. Of all the things I'd been in my life, I couldn't call myself either of those. In a black-and-white world, I was gray as hell.

Famine hated me for some other reason, something compelling enough that she purposely let me see her. She wanted a good look at me, physically and energetically, to size me up. To understand me.

Or she wanted me to see her hatred, to understand her.

Either way, I was in no shape to go up against her directly. If only the Angel and I could use our magic to hurt her badly enough—to shove her far enough away—to shift the odds in the fight. But we couldn't. Not now.

I retreated into the house, stepping backwards over the threshold so as not to take my eyes off of her, shutting the door between us firmly and turning the deadbolt with finality. I didn't have to see her to know that she stayed where she was for a long moment afterward, as if trying to bore a hole through magic and wood to get to me.

"She's out there?" Beth asked.

I nodded.

Chair legs scraped against the tile. I turned my head to see Sunday push back from the table and bristle, ready for a fight.

I shook my head. "Can we talk downstairs?"

Addie swiveled in her seat to meet my gaze. "We should be all right to talk in here, even with that creature outside. The protections are strong enough."

Maybe they were. Maybe they weren't.

I made my way down the hall and into the basement without glancing back. Sunday would bring the others.

Pushing through the veils into the protected circle, I exhaled a breath I hadn't realized I'd been holding. The side door Gabriel had once waltzed through with his feet afire had been barricaded with enough magic to take down a herd of archangels. The stuff of our ordinary lives lay in wait: the washer and dryer, a mountain of towels piled on top; the rainbow of rug and pillows in the center of the room, where so many victories and tragedies had played out.

I felt off-balance. Not surprising, given that I was holding onto my mind, body, and magic by sheer force of power and will. My family was making contingency plans to deal with the aftermath of my transformation or to contain or kill me in the event I gave them no choice. The combined enemy was out there, biding their time. Allies I'd thought we could count on—my grandmother (but not Michael, but I never counted on him)—had betrayed us.

Betrayed me.

I closed my eyes, focusing on my breath, inhaling for four counts and breathing out for six, calming my nervous system and centering my mind and body. It took some effort at the start. My thoughts raced along with the beating of my heart, a cacophony of what-ifs and yes-buts that crashed over me like waves in a storm, relentless, blotting out the night sky and the light of the stars. I couldn't catch my breath. But then the muscle memory of my Order training took over and granted me the ease I desperately needed.

I couldn't count the number of times in my life I'd been knocked off balance or how many of those times had carried the price of my life if I hadn't managed to get my shit together before the next blow. None of them had been this bad. This heartbreaking. This earth-shattering.

No doubt I'd face this again and again from here on out. I had no control over that. No one did, no matter how well trained. No matter how powerful. What I could control was how quickly I returned to center. The faster I got my balance back, the lower the chance I'd end up dead. Or hurting someone I loved.

In the end, that was what I could do, so I did.

My mind calmed. My body responded with a surge of strength. My magic shone, the dark sky of my halo solid.

La Muerte's whispered voice sounded in my depths again. Just one word that mattered so much.

Night.

I listened for more, and when it didn't come, I released the expectation and the desperation I felt. I let it fall away from me. It slipped from my skin in small drops, falling onto the concrete beneath my feet like rain.

The single feather that had moved near my heart fluttered again, and this time I knew it for what it was—a sign that the Angel had not abandoned me, that we were still in this together.

Smaller wings beat within my chest, the size of tiny moths. I'd felt that before. I knew what it meant. This wasn't the Angel, but something else. Or someone else. I pressed the heel of my hand against the skin over my heart.

My heart was not only the source of my life, love, and magic, it contained multitudes. Being one with the Angel meant the ability to carry the souls of the dead and souls that had been somehow separated from their physical bodies. I'd learned that when Luna's soul had taken refuge within me. I'd learned it before Luna and before the Angel, although I hadn't understood, not completely. The soul parts of my long-ago victims, the ones who'd joined to replace the soul I'd killed in my years of bloody vengeance—they lived within me, too. They were alive, and the sensation of moth wings inside told me so.

They told me I wasn't alone. I would never be alone.

A flash of light shifted my consciousness outward again. The portal between the house and Red's gym opened just long enough to dislodge two people I loved and trusted. They looked at me as if I were myself, not a potential enemy. Maybe that was genuine feeling on their part, or maybe they were putting on a show. Either way, in that moment, it meant the world.

Miguel grinned at me, the smile lighting up his brown eyes. He shrugged out of his black leather jacket and tossed it into the inner circle atop a bright blue pillow. He wore black from head to toe, from watch cap to steel-toe boots. I marked a bulge at his ankle and a holstered blade with a black handle at his hip. He'd gone out expecting trouble. Or expecting to return to it.

"Glad to see you're still here," he said.

Stacy gave him the side-eye. Against his black, she looked like a hippie rainbow, her only concession to stealth—or the cold—a borrowed, gray wool cap that hemmed in her unruly blond curls, and a matching coat.

She closed the distance between us, looking me over. Without a word, she gathered me into a hug. She stank of sulfur. The portal passed through the way station between all the worlds, the In-Between.

"What's that for?" I asked.

"In case I don't get to do it again," she said.

I pulled away. "You have any trouble?"

"No attacks. No hiccups. We did reinforce the portals, though, if you're wondering."

Guarding against the In-Between and its diminishing reliability. "Good."

"Where are the others?" she asked.

Footfalls behind me signaled a milling down the stairs. One by one, my family stepped through the veil of protection into the basement. Every last one of them.

Sunday took her usual position by the side door. Even shielded as powerfully as it was, it remained a vulnerability. Doors were made to pass through, a purpose that always tried to reassert itself.

I'd had that same thought, a million years ago, back at the apartment I thought I could make into a home. *La Muerte* and I had warded the door before we'd left. We'd tried to protect what we had and who we loved, but that wasn't our purpose here.

Red made a beeline for me. I held out my hand and he took it, twining his fingers with mine. The steadiness in his eyes and the sure way he held himself told me he'd either dealt with his very real fears or boxed them away to revisit later. Either way, he was here, he was mine, and he had my back. His grass-and-earth halo was filled with strength. The sacred heart on his chest glowed, not ready for battle, but awake.

Faith was right behind him. She was as closed as he was open— hands balled into fists, shoulders tensed and raised halfway to her ears, eyes veiled and halo sparking against anything that might come at her. She expected pain. She'd erected her defenses.

We'd gone up against the End before. We'd battled other threats. But I'd never been the threat before, not like this.

"Promise you won't leave without saying goodbye," she said.

Her words hit me like a punch to the gut.

By "leave," she meant, "merge with the Angel completely." She expected that no trace of me, of who I was, would remain. She expected me to go wherever the Angel of Death would go and not return. She'd said as much to me before. She wasn't worried that the group would fall apart without me—no, she did worry about that.

The heart of her fear was that she would fall apart without me.

It didn't seem like a new fear. It felt old, born the moment she understood that her parents were dead and that I was the only person in all the worlds who stood between her and the forces hunting her.

We each had our purpose. Mine had been to protect her. To finish raising her, undoing as much of the damage her parents had done as I could. To show her by example how to harness her magic and how to measure the consequences of her actions for herself and others. To show her what it meant to love.

She was asking me to do one last thing for her, if and when it came to that.

"I promise."

It was the least I could say or do. I only prayed I'd be able to keep that vow.

She drew a shuddering breath and stepped away, seeking out Corey, who glanced at me with questions in her eyes. *Was Faith all right? Had I given her what she wanted?*

Not what she wanted. What she needed.

I nodded.

The others filed in. We filled the circle of pillows, everyone taking a seat without another word. The basement filled with the sounds of cracking joints and the whisper of breath, anticipation rising and sharpening like a knife's edge, ready to cut. Ready for blood.

Addie settled on a cushion directly across from mine. She looked at me, her expression warring between rage and nothing at all in an attempt to hide her feelings.

She broke the silence. "Tell us what you've come to say."

CHAPTER 11

FROM THE LOOK on Addie's face—the sorrow in her dark brown eyes, the pale undertone of her brown skin, the straight set of her mouth—she already knew what I planned to say. Her halo was so full of stars, I could hardly see the velvet black of it, and every single one of those stars pulsed and vibrated as if they might explode any second, taking out the basement, the house above it, and everyone and everything within.

I scanned the faces of the others. Ben, his halo solid gray stone, his eyes wary and unsure. Jess obviously feeling the vibes flowing from her aunt, fidgeting in front of Ben and staring at her hands. Stacy, the indigo of her halo a deep pool with no bottom. And Miguel, his expression and his expectations empty, waiting to be filled, waiting to shape-shift into whatever might be needed. Faith and Corey, hand in hand, vibrating with nerves. Beth, arms folded across her chest.

None of them knew, but Addie did.

"I can't stay here."

Four simple syllables that carried the weight of the world.

Red's grip on my hand tightened enough to strangle the blood supply. Before he could breathe a word, Faith shot from where she'd folded herself into Corey's arms, her brown eyes wild, so many sparks dripping from her fingertips, they could set the rug on fire.

"No," she said.

It carried every ounce of her will and every prayer she'd ever whispered in the dark. She would not allow me to leave. She refused. Every piece of her infused the word, but the god she carried had not added his power to her voice.

I took a deep breath. "Hear me out."

She shook her head.

She'd told me what she feared, and I was feeding it to her like poison fruit. Like an evil stepmother with a shiny apple in hand. I offered her my absence and, with it, she would fall apart. I offered her my death, because Famine and the End would come after me, and how could I possibly survive out there on my own? That was what I meant to do, right—go out on my own?

Ben cleared his throat, his deep voice slicing through the pain in the air. "You wouldn't leave any of us here without your firepower. That would make us sitting ducks. You would never do that."

"She wouldn't," Stacy said. "She'd send us away, though."

Miguel nodded. "The back door into Faery. The one we just secured in case we needed an escape route."

"That's bullshit," Faith said. "After everything we've been through, it's not right."

Miguel searched her face, his own flushing with thought and strategy. With purpose. "We do what the fight demands of us."

"I'm not an Order operative," she said. "I don't have to play by your rules."

"You're the daughter of one. You have eyes to see what's been going on here all this time. You have power—Jesus, you have more power than all the rest of us. You carry the goddamn source of all magic. You have to grow up, Faith. You've been doing an admirable job, and in a perfect world you'd have more time. But the world isn't perfect. There's no right. There's no fair. There's only what is. Got that?"

"Fuck you, Miguel." Faith trembled, her body vibrating with emotion.

He started to respond, but caught my eye and held back.

Faith felt too much and there was nowhere for all of that feeling to go. He was right, but what he'd said was harsh, and she needed a minute to take it in, to remember that he was her friend, to understand.

Right now, the sparks falling from her fingertips became streams of flame. The stink of burning jute filled the space.

Corey rose behind Faith, grabbed her by the shoulders, and marched her toward Sunday, stopping only once they'd cleared the rug. Faith's fire couldn't hurt the concrete floor—at least, not in its current state. If she got hot enough to kill, that would be a different story.

Corey bent close, her red hair hiding her face, but the word she spoke softly into Faith's ear was clear as a blue sky.

"Breathe."

Faith did the opposite, holding her breath like a small child desperate enough to pass out rather than deal. I knew exactly how she felt.

Red let go of my hand. He started to move around the circle toward them, but I stretched out an arm to stall him. If anyone was going to get hurt here, it would be me. I was the one who'd caused the pain, and if Faith lashed out, I would take what she threw at me.

I made my way over, gliding in close enough to risk the heat. Close enough for Faith to know I was there—that I wanted to be there.

After a moment, she inhaled and glanced up to meet my gaze. "You're not leaving us. You're taking the fight to them. You don't want them to attack the house, or the neighborhood around it. People would die."

"That's one reason," I said.

"They want you, not us." She mulled that for a moment. "But if they do want us, you want their forces split. Multiple fronts to the fight. Threats in proportion to what we can handle."

I nodded.

"There's no guarantee that things will play out the way you plan," she said.

"There never is, Faith. In fact, things almost never go how I plan."

"Then how do you decide?"

"I make the best plan I can and then deal with what comes up. That's all any of us can do." I stole a glimpse at Beth.

She winked at me.

Faith understood what I'd told her. She just didn't like it. "Your magic is all wrong right now."

"It won't be that way for long."

She didn't revisit the inevitable transformation or her fears. She rubbed the heel of her hand against her heart, scorching her top. "Then you'll be able to do what you need to."

Whatever that meant for all of us. "Yes."

"I'm coming with you."

As her mother, my instinct was to say no. A thousand times, no. As an operative? We needed her power and her heart on our team.

"You can't go alone," she said.

I heard the hopes and fears behind those words. What she'd said and what she meant—that I shouldn't fight by myself, and I shouldn't go through this transformation on my own. I would leave her, but she refused to leave me alone.

I couldn't bring myself to say the word she longed to hear. It stuck in my throat, throbbing there. But it needed to be spoken somehow.

I nodded.

The fire went out of her as if I'd flipped a switch. The flame in her fingers receded, and she stopped shaking. She drew a deeper breath. Her cheeks flushed with color, and her halo dimmed.

She closed her eyes for a moment. When she looked at me again, she didn't seem scared of the fight to come or impending death or doom. She seemed at peace.

"Thank you," she said.

Sunday walked toward us, folding her arms across her chest. "Now that we can be sure you won't blow us up anytime soon, Faith, we should all talk."

Faith met her gaze. "Sorry, not sorry."

Sunday rolled her eyes, all sarcasm on the outside, but deadly serious. "The plan was for Night to go alone and for the rest of us to hide in Faery."

I found my voice. "It's a good plan."

"Genius," she said. "Except for the stupid part."

I raised a brow.

"If we're in Faery, we can't help you, Night. The last time we went up against the End, it took all of us—all of our magic, combined—to toast his ass. You think it's going to be any different now? If so, tell us why and show your work, because I call bullshit."

"The Angel—"

She waved me off. "The Angel is exactly who he's always been. Maybe if he takes over, you're more powerful, but maybe not. We can't take that chance. There will be no suicide missions happening on my watch."

Suicide? "That's not what I—"

"Not consciously, no. But what else would you call going up against the king of destruction? He's so powerful that, regardless of what we do now, he'll win when it's all said and done. The world will eventually end. Everything will go dark, and he'll have the nothing and no one he wants. And we haven't even gotten to Famine yet."

"I'm more powerful than she is," I said.

"But you can't kill her, am I right? None of you Horsemen can be killed. So what are you planning to do with her? Take her out of commission? Incapacitate her? Tie her up and drop her in Addie's basement?"

I stared at her.

"Not to speak for Addie, but I'm not sure she thinks that's a great idea. And it won't be enough. Famine's wily. She's been doing this a lot longer than you, and she'll find a way out. Then what?"

I held up a hand to stop the avalanche, but she barreled through.

"I won't allow it, and if you think I can't stop you because you've got Angel juice, think again, my friend."

"Are you finished?" I asked.

She mulled the question. "Yes."

Sunday never talked to me as if I were stupid. I'd considered every point she'd brought and then some, and she was one-hundred-percent right in the conclusions she'd pummeled me with. She hadn't touched on the alternatives because she couldn't see them. She was just as scared as Faith and me, and beating me black-and-blue with her words was her way of showing it.

Normally, the idea of Sunday afraid would give me pause. She'd been a better operative than I was. She was faster, smarter, stronger. But her record and her strengths might not put us over the top in this fight, and she knew it.

We all did. We all felt what she did.

I would have to agree not to go alone, or even just with Faith, because if I tried to do that, the others would follow. I wouldn't be able to convince them not to, and I wouldn't force them via magic. That would only jeopardize their ability to defend themselves.

Sunday read all of that on my face. Her lips curved. "Good. Now that we've got that settled, we can talk about the plan we're actually going to follow."

Addie, tired of looking over her shoulder, spun slowly on her pillow, turning to face us. "Does this plan involve an archangel?"

"It might," I said.

"The one I couldn't get to answer me awhile ago?"

I nodded.

"What makes you think you'll have better luck?" she asked. "Please tell me you didn't plan to throw yourself off a cliff with Famine and the End and count on Michael to save you."

"Has he ever shown up for me when I needed him?" I asked. "Why would I count on that?"

She cocked her head, studying me.

Red raised his hands as if to hold back the tide. "Wait."

Sunday shook her head. "No time to waste, Jennings."

He spoke through clenched teeth. "Wait just a goddamn minute."

She bit back whatever sarcastic response she intended to make. "What did we miss? What do you see that we don't?"

"This is the end of everything," he said.

"Have a little faith, Red."

"I do." He combed his fingers through his hair, fisting his hands in it. "That's the problem, isn't it?"

I met his gaze, the green of his eyes bright and sharp as a knife's edge. I read everything he hadn't said in his face and in the pull of the heart link we shared.

He'd been with me every step of the way since we'd become part of each other's lives again, been present for every battle, been there to see the objective done and that I came out the other end alive and as whole as possible. This time was different. This time, he couldn't come with me, and it was killing him.

I tugged at his heart, letting him know that I knew, making sure he knew how I felt.

He sighed. "Show of hands—who's going with Night?"

Sunday and Faith. Miguel.

Ben rolled from his seat into a squat, rocking on the balls of his feet. "We should set up something like we had last time we went up against the End. A conduit to feed you our magic if you need it."

"That will make you vulnerable," I said. "Taking the portal into Faery is safer."

He shrugged. "Yeah, but I don't care. I don't want to speak for anyone else here, but I'm betting they don't either. We've come too far. Risked too much. We've still got too much to lose to stand on the sidelines now."

Beside him, Jess leaned forward, resting her elbows on her knees. "We should be smart about it. The basement is the logical place to set up, but we need to have the portal to the gym open, and we need to have the portal to Faery ready to go from there. If we can make a difference, we make it, no matter what happens. If we've used up our shot, we retreat. Can we all agree to that?"

I glanced around the room. Nods all around.

"We're settled, then," I said.

"When do we leave?" Faith asked.

"Tonight," I said.

"Just after midnight," Addie amended.

I canted my head. "Why?"

"There's something I want to do first, and midnight is the best time. Corey, honey? I'm going to need your help."

Corey looked like a deer in the headlights. "Mine?"

"Yes, ma'am." Addie pushed to her feet. "I'm going to cook us something, some special magic for the road. Everyone except Corey is banished from the kitchen until I call you. Understand?"

No one objected. No one would dare.

Addie led the march up the stairs and back into the real world, where full dark had set in, leaving us hemmed in by our own magical protections and alone in our sea of electric lights.

I followed Red to our room, snicking the door shut behind us. For a heartbeat, we stood in the pitch black. Then he flicked the switch on the bathroom wall, bracing his hands on the sides of the sink, head down.

I couldn't see his face behind the silver-and-black curtain of his hair. The muscles of his arms bunched beneath his sleeves, as if he were holding on for dear life. I closed the distance between us until I was near enough to touch him.

"I'd counted on more time," he said softly.

"If we wait for the enemy to attack, we might have days. Or we might have hours. And they'd kill every single one of us who's capable of dying. Their power combined is too much."

"I know all that." He pushed away from the sink. "Just like I know that right now is the only sure thing. It's always been the only thing."

I lifted my hands, resting my palms against his chest. At my touch, the glow of his sacred heart grew stronger.

"That's you, you know," he said.

I shook my head. "It's who you are."

"I'm in there, sure. I don't even know what this magic is—not entirely. I only know what it does to me. I can't close off my heart, Night. I can't put up walls or shields. I can only feel. That didn't start with me. It started with you. You cracked my heart open."

I held his gaze. "No, that's what you did to me—and more than that. I loved exactly one person when you hired me: Faith. I didn't know how to open up. I was too afraid. I didn't trust myself. I didn't know how to get past the terrible things I did with the Order. And before the Order, with my parents. I thought I'd killed them. I thought I was a monster. You changed all of that."

He absorbed my words like a man dying of thirst who's found a pool of water. I felt him through the heart link. It was too much to drink in at once.

"I want to ask you the same thing I asked last time," he said. "I want you to promise you'll come back to me."

I wanted to be able to promise that more than anything in the world. I started to say so.

He shook his head, cutting me off. "Let me get this out."

I waited.

"I realized downstairs that I can't ask you to do that. You said before that if we stayed here and waited for the bastards to attack, we might have days or we might have hours. We would never have days, Night. I can see what you can't—or won't. The magic you're working on yourself to keep moving, to keep your systems running in the face of the change that's happening inside, is burning you up too fast. You have tonight. Maybe part of tomorrow. After that, everything will be different."

The end of everything.

I didn't want to look too closely at what Dream's actions had wrought. At how much juice I had left. How long I could keep going this way. How long I could keep the transformation at bay. And I didn't have to. I knew he was right. I knew it in my marrow.

He tripped over the next words. "You don't...have even as long as...tomorrow. When you need your magic to fight, you'll have to strip yourself down all the way to have a prayer. You'll be running on empty then. You'll be done. Part of me is glad not to be going, because how could I watch that happen to you without it tearing me apart inside? But the rest of me, it needs to be there, because I can't let you change or...die...alone. Do you understand that, Night? Please tell me you understand."

I wrapped my arms around him, burying my face in the light and warmth of his chest. I did that as much to hide the tears that threatened as to show him that I got it. I got him.

He kissed the crown of my head, breathing in my scent.

"When I breathe you in, I'm breathing in your magic," I said. "Grass and earth. Solid and strong."

He bent to whisper in my ear. "You smell like the night to me—the way it smelled back home. Brine from the Gulf of Mexico in the air and humidity so thick that moving through it felt like walking through molasses. The surprise of a breeze rattling the branches of oaks."

A spark rolled through me from crown to heart, blazing to life as it landed.

"And something else," he said. "Roses. Red and ripe and full of velvet promise."

I tried to pull back so I could look at him. I needed to memorize the way he looked in that moment. He tightened his hold on me, drawing me so close, I couldn't tell where he ended and I began.

"We don't have enough time," he said. "But I'll take what I can get and I won't regret that there's not more. Can you do that with me?"

I nodded.

He stepped away, cupping his hand under my chin and tilting my head back so that I could catch that glimpse of him that I needed so badly. The green of his eyes had darkened like leaves after a hard rain. I committed their color to memory—and the lines that etched his forehead, the sharp lines and curves of his face, the shape of his mustache, and the magic of his mouth.

I took his face in my hands and brushed my lips across his, watching him all the while. He watched me, too, finally closing his eyes as he deepened the kiss, drinking me in. His fingertips skimming the sides of my breasts and the curve of my waist before sliding between my jeans and my belly, searching for a way in.

I reached for the hem of his shirt and tugged. He raised his arms and pulled the rest of the way, giving me access to his skin. The glow of the flaming heart on his chest shone blindingly bright. He shivered as I trailed my knuckles down the flat plane of his stomach, reaching for the button and zipper of his jeans.

He took my hand before I could wrap it around him, twining his fingers with mine. "Not yet."

I quirked a brow.

His mouth curved into a smile. "You want to see me? I want to see you."

I tried not to hear the rest of that sentence, but it hung between us. *Because I might never see you again. Not like this.*

He studied my face, tracing every line, every curve. Holding up under that scrutiny—the intimacy of it—was harder than anything I'd done before. His gaze stripped every single defense bare, entering into every emotion I carried in my heart, tasting every decision that had brought me to this moment, highlighting every fear and hope, joy and sorrow, reducing me to the one thing that mattered most.

Love.

Everything I loved: the gym and the kids who'd walked through the door and allowed me to help them. The heat of posole and the now-tainted memories of *mi abuelita*. The warmth of the sun on my face and the chill of clouds and rain. The taste of coffee and whiskey. The strain of my muscles in the midst of the action and the languid, liquid pleasure of sleeping beside him.

Everyone I loved: Faith, for who she was and who she might become, for daring to love me even after she understood how much I'd taken from her and why. Sunday, for giving me a home to run to inside the Order, for the heart she hid behind sarcasm and bravado, for her fearlessness. The rest of my family here for all their strengths and challenges, for their willingness to fight a battle no matter the cost. Even Addie. Even Beth.

Red, from the moment he'd taken me in on the night my parents died, keeping me safe and out of sight until the immediate danger had passed, never asking a single thing of me in return. For opening his door to me when I'd arrived in Portland, for not asking questions until he had no choice. For his ability to understand and wrap his mind and heart around who I once was and who I was now. For not allowing the fact that we were unlikely to get out of this fight alive to stop him from going all in.

He spoke softly. "Is that all?"

I shook my head. "For the way you are in the world, with everyone. How you see their beauty and strength, especially when all they can see are their faults. For the way you protect them, sometimes even from themselves. And that you do it because it's right, because it's who you are, and because every one of them is vital and gorgeous and you won't let them fall if it's the last thing you do."

He kissed me, drawing me in deep. His hands moved at my waist, making quick work of the button and zipper on my jeans, pulling my shirt over my head, making me as naked on the outside as I felt inside. Instinctively, I held my wings as close as I could, making them smaller, wishing them away.

He shook his head. "I want all or nothing, Night."

I held my breath.

"All of who you are, or nothing at all."

I let my wings unfurl. As they did, my magic rose, crackling at my edges. In that moment, I felt more angel than human, more unlike myself than I ever had. But he didn't look at me as if I'd become an alien. He looked at me as if I were the only thing in the world he loved. Wave after wave of power rolled through me as if I were a star in the sky, burning from the inside out.

"That's more like it." He lifted me high.

I wrapped my legs around his waist as he carried me around the corner to the bed. He laid me down gently, wings spread beneath me. He bent to taste the skin of my belly, sliding his arms beneath my thighs as his lips trailed downward, and then I ceased to see or feel anything except his mouth on me. Wave after wave of pleasure crashed over me, the star fire inside growing brighter until it exploded across my skin, incandescent.

When he pulled away, it felt like desertion. Like bereavement. When he closed his mouth over mine, it was like coming home. I never wanted to leave.

He brushed the hair from my face, holding my gaze. "You're not."

"I'm not what?" I asked.

"Leaving. We're in this together, no matter what happens."

I prayed by all the powers that what he said was true.

"What is it?" he asked.

Prayers would have to do, because all we had was now. I pushed away every worry that wanted to intrude if only I allowed them.

"You didn't let me finish before," I said. "There was more."

"Tell me."

"I love you for the way you touch me. For the way I feel when you slide into me and the way we move together. For the glimpse of your depths when you look into my eyes. I love the way you smell, the way you taste—your magic, your skin, your sex."

I loved the weight of him on top of me. And underneath me.

I rolled him over onto his back, pinning his wrists above his head, and kissed him until he could barely breathe. I took my time tasting the salt and grass and earth of his skin—the hollow of his throat, the sacred heart on his chest, the holy length of his stomach, the sweetness of his thighs.

This time, he let me wrap my hand around his cock, sucking in a breath as I took him into my mouth. He took everything I gave, hands fisted first in the sheets and then in my hair, drawing me up to kiss me with the last of his control. Then it was his turn to roll me onto my back, to slide a knee between my legs.

He pressed a palm over my heart. "Look at me, Night."

I locked my gaze with his.

"I need something from you," he said.

"Tell me."

"Wrap us in your wings."

I'd only done that to protect. To shield.

Looking into his eyes, I saw straight through to his soul. He showed me everything, and I understood that protection was exactly what he wanted from me. He wanted there to be only the two of us just this once.

"All or nothing," I said.

His mouth was hot and demanding on mine. He poured all of himself into me.

I stretched my wings to their full size, and they took the shape I asked them to, spiraling around our bodies, lifting elbows and knees with their passage, kissing skin and magic. Feathers and shadow blotted out the world, shielding us from everything except one another, leaving us in darkness except for the glow of his sacred heart and the starlight of my changing magic.

The heart link opened wide. I felt everything he did, and I knew he felt every emotion, every sensation that I did when he entered me.

We moved together, the rhythm of our bodies a heartbeat so strong and so enormous, it swallowed us whole. Every thrust, every kiss, every touch burned, joining us until we were no longer two, but one. One body. One heart. One soul.

He slid a hand up my spine, palm behind my heart, and lifted me, pulling me close. I met his gaze—and he met mine—as we came, diving deep into one another. He held me there afterwards, whispering my name, heart racing and breath ragged.

"I love you," he said when he could speak again.

I kissed his damp brow, drawing his head down to my chest. He fought me for a second, then gave in. I stroked his hair, feeling tears hot and wild rise within me, refusing to let them run.

Blocking out the world only worked for so long, especially when the enemy was not only outside, but inside as well.

I managed to keep my voice steady. "I love you, too."

"How long can we stay here like this?"

"As long as we want."

He grinned. "Liar."

"Awhile," I amended.

After a moment, he let me know I hadn't fooled him. "Are you here with me, Night?"

I nodded.

"Then let it out. I promise I can take it." He raised his head to look at me, tugging at the heart link.

That pull was all it took.

The tears tumbled out of me, searing and raw. He wrapped his arms around me while they raged. He didn't let go until I pulled back, then he wiped away the remains of the storm with his fingertips.

He kissed me with so much tenderness, it broke my heart.

I needed to go. To get ready to face the enemy. To face myself.

He read the shift in me before I said a word.

"Just a little while longer," he said.

I could give him that.

He stroked the curve of my breast and hip, the inside of my thigh. I opened for him like a flower blooming in the morning sun.

Just a little while longer.

CHAPTER 12

WHATEVER SECRET MAGIC Addie and Corey had been up to in the kitchen, they'd finished and gone. Sunday waited for me in the darkened room, a shadow in the chair closest to the back door.

The light from the small bulb under the stove hood didn't reach her, but it did touch the fresh pot of coffee she'd brewed and the plate of cheese and sliced apples she'd made up for me. I thought I had too many butterflies in my belly to eat, but the sight of food made me realize how damn hungry I was.

The clock on the wall ticked mercilessly forward. Ten-thirty-two and counting. An hour and a half until launch.

As my eyes adjusted, I marked Sunday's silhouette more clearly. And that of the knife she twirled with her right hand, the tip of its blade spinning on Addie's old oak table.

"You put a hole in that wood, Addie's gonna kick your ass," I said, shoving a chunk of Gouda into my mouth.

"Do you really think there'll be anything left of me when we're done, much less my ass?"

I reached for a mug from the cabinet. "You'd better hope so."

"I'll take my hope one step at a time, thanks."

I slid into the seat next to hers, inclining my head toward the plate. "Thanks for this."

"You sure you want to take Faith with us?" she asked.

Small talk was over.

"She's untested," Sunday said.

"She's a god."

"She's not part of our unit. We have a flow."

"She'll learn," I said.

"But what if—"

"Something happens to me and she's there to see it?"

Sunday frowned.

"I understand," I said. "I've thought about it until I was one-hundred-percent certain my brain would bleed."

"Okay," she said.

"Okay? That's it?" I took a swig of coffee. "Why does it matter, Sunday?"

"Because, contrary to my pessimism, I want to live. And because I love you and I love her."

And because if Sunday lived, she would be the one sweeping up the shards of Faith's shattered heart. I didn't have to ask her. She and Red would take in Faith and Corey and anyone else I loved.

Sunday sighed. "Any last words?"

"You already know them."

Knuckles rapped on the doorframe. Miguel slipped into the room and took the chair at the end of the table, flipped it around, and straddled the seat. He looked mission-ready, armed to the teeth, his steps soundless on the tile, the purple in his bruised halo light as mist.

"I've been turning things over in my head," he said. "Michael first, then straight to the End."

Sunday nodded. "Let Famine think she has our flank."

"She's won't buy it," I said.

"Nope. But she will try to take advantage of it if we leave ourselves vulnerable long enough. And then Beth—"

Faith's voice wafted from the hall. "What am I supposed to be doing while all this happens?"

Miguel leaned back, wrapping his fingers around the seatback. "No need to eavesdrop, kiddo. You're one of us."

She marched in, flipping on the lights.

The three of us winced.

"I want to see your faces," she said. "And I'm not a kid. Not anymore."

Her fingertips glowed as if they were on fire, but she held the sparks at bay. Her silver-and-gold halo bled into her silver-and-gold sweater. Not the stealthiest battle wear, but we didn't need her to be invisible. Just the opposite, in fact.

Jesus Christ.

If Faith was going to have a hope in hell in all of this, it couldn't just be about whether or not she would come with us, or whether she had the juice to hold her own. The mother in me would have to be subsumed by the operative. I needed to push the smart play. The one with the best chance of success.

I set my mind on that. I set my heart on it. I turned the page.

"You heard what Miguel said?" I asked.

"All of it."

"What do you think?" I asked.

"That you want me to deal with Famine."

I shook my head. "No, I need you with me."

"To keep an eye on me?"

She was the most powerful among us—Miguel was right. The Awakened was pure creation, pure magic. The End was annihilation of everything the Awakened stood for. Fire and water. Matter and anti-matter.

"To go up against the End."

"Oh." Her eyes widened. She searched my face, glimpsing the gleam in my eyes, then moved on to Sunday's.

Sunday nodded her approval.

Faith took that in, smoothing her sweater and jeans with surprisingly steady hands. If Sunday thought it was a good idea—if Sunday believed she could do it—then Faith would do everything in her power to make it happen.

Faith thought Sunday was objective where she was concerned. It was fine that she didn't know any better.

Miguel laced his fingers together, popping his knuckles. "We're set."

Faith blinked. "Wait—what? That's not a plan. That's an outline. A loose outline."

"That's how it works," he said.

"But you'll tell me what to do when the time comes."

"Probably not, kid—Faith."

"Then how will I know?"

"The same way we do," Sunday said. "Pay attention to what's going on around you. If you can see us, watch what we do and then take the action that makes the most sense. Keep the goal in mind."

"Staying alive," she said. "Pushing the enemy back enough to get us breathing room."

I shook my head. "No."

"But that's what makes sense," Faith said.

"The order has always been: One, push the enemy back. Two, keep the rest of you alive. Three, keep myself alive if I can."

She stared at me.

"Sometimes you have to risk everything to win," I said.

She echoed me. "Everything."

"The goal this time is to risk everything."

"But the End, Famine—they can't be killed."

"They can be hurt," I said. "If we hurt them badly enough—if we beat them within an inch of death—the breathing room we get could be our whole lives."

"And if that doesn't work?"

Sunday spun her blade on its tip. "Then the goal shifts. We cut our losses. Retreat."

"By losses, you mean people?" Faith asked.

Sunday didn't answer. She didn't need to.

Faith backpedaled a couple of steps, leaning into the wall and sliding her hands into her front pockets. "You know, when I was on the outside—keeping back, waiting for the cavalry to come home—I had this glorious, romantic picture of what the three of you were doing."

"It's not romantic," Sunday said.

Miguel's mouth quirked into a half-grin. "It's bloody."

"You like it," Faith said.

"'Like' is a strong word," I said. "It's what we were made for. You're my child in spirit, if not in blood. In the same way, we are the Order's children. No matter how long we've been out and how far away we've run, a fight like this feels like coming home."

She rolled her eyes, the simple gesture meant to mask fear. It didn't work, but all three of us let her have it.

"Y'all have lost your minds," she said.

Miguel shrugged. Sunday chuckled.

I nodded. "It's all or nothing."

Faith mulled that for a moment, then pointed herself at the coffeepot. As she took her first sip, Stacy poked her head into the kitchen, her frizzy blond curls tamed by a violet headband.

"We're ready downstairs," she said. "If you're planning to, you know, summon anyone, you should get on it."

She didn't wait for an acknowledgement, ducking out as suddenly as she'd appeared.

I met Miguel's gaze. "You ready?"

His half-smile grew to a full-on grin. "Where are we doing this?"

"Right here," I said.

Sunday's eyebrows climbed all the way to her hairline. "Addie's going to kill me for marking up her table? You're summoning an archangel in her fucking kitchen. He's going to get his fire and wrath all over everything."

"Thank you, Captain Sarcasm."

"That's General Sarcasm to you, Sanchez." She pushed away from the table, rising to her feet and sliding the blade into its sheath at her waist. "You want privacy?"

"No," I said, pushing to my feet.

I closed my eyes.

The insides of my lids glowed with star fire.

It was all I could do to take that in stride, here in the house where I felt safest, where I'd put all of my effort into slowing down the change that Dream had sped up. The fire behind my eyes was the first sign that Red was right. I didn't have long before *La Muerte* and I transformed.

I drew a deep breath and blew it out on a long count, then again. Four in, six out, until my spiked nerves calmed and I could focus my mind. The feathers surrounding my heart stirred, answering my attention.

I spoke the Angel's name silently.

He expanded to fill my skin, his magic pulsing with my breath. *I'm here.*

A tumble of thoughts threatened to supplant the words I wanted to speak. *I'm scared. How long until there is no more me and no more you, just us? Will I be able to finish what I've started?*

I marshaled my will and bound those threats, shoving them behind the first door that showed itself within my mind and locking them in tight.

We need Michael, I said.

The Angel's face bloomed within my darkness, so close it was as if I were gazing into his eyes, as if I could feel his breath on my cheek, as if he were a fraction of a second from being born into the world, erasing me utterly from existence. The same star fire behind my eyes burned in his.

I opened my mouth to speak. The voice that issued forth was not mine, nor was it the Angel's. It was ours.

"Michael."

Just the one word, but woven within it were the flames of the archangel's fiery sword. The signature of his power.

The Angel moved our legs, adjusting them wide and stable, then taking a step forward before planting our feet and spreading our wings to full width, shielding the others from what was about to happen.

The space between us and the hall door blazed with light so bright, it seared my skin. Instinctively, I tried to shut my eyes against it, but the Angel willed them open, so I saw every molecule of the air vibrate and then displace, as if they'd slid into another dimension to make room for the being that took their place.

He materialized from the tips of his great wings to the powerful muscle of his shoulders, from his many fiery eyes to his golden hair, from the sword sheathed at his back to his powerful torso and legs. As all of him arrived, the light began to dim, turning my world into a photo negative for a heartbeat—light where darkness ought to be, and darkness in place of light.

The heat of him was immense. Sweat broke on my forehead. The fine hairs on my arms singed. The air felt too hot to breathe. If I drew it in, it would burn every passage through which it passed. Everything it touched.

Addie's tile floor was a goner. Hopefully, the rest of the room would survive.

Michael was so much larger than he appeared, larger than the room, and the house, and the neighborhood. His form could fill all of Portland if he wanted. He made himself smaller, though no less powerful, for our sake.

He changed, taking on the form familiar to me. Black hair, golden eyes, denim jacket and jeans. Black T-shirt with *Ride the Lightning* splashed across the front. The air bent around him, and now that I'd had a glimpse of his true form, I understood why in a visceral way.

His voice held a touch of anger. "What did I tell you?"

"Not to call you for help," I said. "I'm not."

He raised a brow.

"It's not how you can help me," I said. "It's how I can help you."

At that, he eased his light so as not to blind—or incinerate—the humans in the room.

The Angel and I folded our wings.

Michael studied the team, scrutiny lingering on each of them, from Faith to Sunday to Miguel.

"You're joking, aren't you?" Michael asked. "A chameleon?"

"Do I look like I'm joking?"

He met my gaze. "Why would you do this?"

"You want in on this fight, but you're not allowed to join it," I said.

At that, he threw back his head and laughed. "You're full of surprises."

"I like to think I'm practical," I said. "The question is, will it work?"

He wagged a finger at Miguel, who didn't hesitate to step forward.

Michael looked him up and down, eyes narrowed. "You were made a chameleon by the Order, but after that they did something else to you. They made you into a container."

"For the Angel of Death," Miguel said.

The Order had trained him and prepared him to be what I was. They'd given him the magical structure to house the Angel, but they couldn't give him the one thing that would allow him to hold the Angel long-term: an archangel's blood flowing through his veins.

"You came here to copy me," Michael said.

"That's what I do. What I am."

"What if I made you a different offer?"

Miguel stared at him.

"Not the one you're thinking," Michael said. "It's tempting to consider joining the battle by joining with you. I could do what I wanted and the powers that have forbidden me to act would be none the wiser. You wouldn't survive housing me for more than an hour and you'd be irreparably damaged well before then, and we need you in the fight."

"That's supposed to make me feel better?" Miguel asked.

"It should."

Because deciding a man's fate as if he were a pawn on a chessboard always made a guy feel better.

Miguel scowled.

The archangel waved him off, dismissing his feelings as if they didn't matter. Which to Michael, they didn't.

"There may come a time when you need me," Michael said. "Not a copy of me, but me. If you want me to be there when it counts, I'll need a door into you. Will you give one to me?"

Miguel mulled the question. "Why would you make me that offer? No, I get why you want the option to take the wheel or blast a motherfucker in an emergency, especially if you can do it without getting caught. But why not use Night for that? She's your descendant. You won't run the risk of hurting her."

I wondered the same thing. I had my own answer, but wanted to hear Michael's.

His gaze grazed my face, the corner of his mouth twitching. "Night already has two people in there. A third would be overcrowding."

My thought exactly, but there was something else, something Michael hadn't said out loud. He hadn't lied, but he hadn't told the whole truth, either.

If Michael had said all of this to me, I'd want days to decide. Now that I knew even a little about what housing a being like the Angel meant, I'd want at least that much time to consider all the angles, to make sure that I was doing what needed to be done, that I had no other choice.

It hadn't worked out that way for me. I'd made a split-second decision to save Faith from this fate, and now I had to live with the consequences. It was more than never being alone again inside my own head, or having enough magical juice to go up against my enemies and win, or the Angel stitching my body back together after those enemies shredded it bloody, or goddamn wings growing out of my back, or losing every ounce of humanity I'd worked so hard to rebuild. It was all of those things combined, with the added bonus of losing everyone I loved and dying.

All of that from a split-second decision that I'd make again in a heartbeat, every single minute of every day.

Miguel looked at the archangel and spoke through clenched teeth. "I give you that door in, I expect you to abide by my red lines."

Michael inclined his head. "Go on."

"You ask permission first unless I'm unconscious. You stay only as long as absolutely necessary and I have the final say on what's necessary. You can't use me to do something I have moral objections to, or harm anyone I love unless there's no other choice, and I define when that is. You leave me better than how you found me."

"A complete list," Michael said. "Agreed."

No hesitation. No argument. In my experience, Michael didn't take orders from anyone, at least not anyone human. So what was this about?

Michael looked at me, his eyes filled with something I never thought I'd see in them: compassion. Coming from him, I had no idea how to feel about that other than suspicious.

"We do what is necessary," he said.

He didn't tell me to leave it alone in so many words, but that was what he meant.

"I want one more thing," Miguel said. "An angel feather."

"No," Michael said.

"But—"

"I agreed to your terms," Michael said. "Deal or no deal?"

Miguel sighed. "Deal."

The word came down like a judge's gavel on the bench, or a hammer on the head of a pin. The finality in it rang like a bell through the room.

That was that. This was between them, and it was done. We had bigger problems to deal with now than Michael.

"Anything else?" I asked. "Anyone else we need to bring in?"

Sunday shook her head. "We're good. Miguel, you got what you need from this asshole?"

Michael furrowed his brow.

"If you're not going to smite me, find someone else to scowl at," Sunday said. "Miguel?"

Miguel bit back a laugh. "I need a few more minutes."

"Michael, why don't you come down to the basement with us?" I asked. "Will that do the trick?"

"All the tricks," Miguel said.

The archangel nodded.

We filed downstairs, Faith in the lead and Miguel and the archangel following, walking close enough to each other for Miguel to siphon critical information about Michael's magic and manner and incorporate them into his own changeable infrastructure. They didn't speak, or even glance at one another.

Sunday and I brought up the rear. She slowed her pace to fall back a little, and I followed suit.

She cocked her head toward the chameleon and the archangel. "That's fucked up."

"Agreed," I said.

"I've got a bad feeling, Night."

"I know how you feel."

She reached for my hand. I twined my fingers with hers. A surge of love coursed through me. She had my back—she would always have my back. She'd embraced the rest of my family as her own. Like Red, she was my home.

"I need you to come in," she said.

She never asked me to invade her mental space. Not once in the entire time I'd known her, not even in the depths of the Order when every word we said aloud might be overheard.

With all of the changes happening inside, I didn't have to ask my magic to rise. It answered before I opened the way. I slipped into Sunday's mind, into a space she'd prepared for the conversation.

Our room at the Order.

A double bed with rumpled sheets and a single gray wool blanket, simple pine stands on either side. A dresser with a plain mirror on the opposite wall, beside it a small closet lit with a bare overhead bulb. A bathroom in the corner, too small for two. No art on the walls. No expansive self-expression at all. It was too dangerous to be honest about who you were in that place, but somehow, we managed.

The collection of pebbles Sunday kept by her side of the bed, brought home from the riverside where we'd passed our first survival test and been allowed to live. The Our Lady of Guadalupe medallion I'd stolen from the scene of my first kill because it reminded me of my mother. Our only sentimental possessions.

We'd saved the rest of our self-expression for each other, stories told in late-night whispers branded on each other's skin with lips and fingertips.

It felt the same. It smelled the same, like shampoo and soap and sex and nightmares.

The two of us standing here after everything we'd been through—we were so much more now.

Why here? I asked.

She slid her hands into her front pockets. *It's a good memory in a bad place.*

Shelter from the storm.

She nodded. *We need a contingency,* she said. *It won't be enough this time to wing it when things go pear-shaped. I get that you've been the contingency since the Angel darkened your door, but—*

I get it. I didn't need her to spell it out. *The Faery King. Kevin's expecting everyone who stays behind in the event of a breach or some other catastrophe.*

He's good, but he might not be enough, at least not alone.

There was only one other among our allies who wielded more power than Kevin. I wanted to say no—hell no—but I bit my tongue. I didn't like Malek and I didn't trust him to do things my way. If we had no other choice?

As a last resort, I said.

She breathed out her relief.

Why hide that you're asking me?

It's not just you, Night. No one wants him here. We're monsters—okay, mostly reformed monsters—but he's worse.

I couldn't argue with that. *Why bother asking me at all? If it comes down to it and I'm out of commission, you'll do whatever it takes.* Without hesitation. Without regrets.

You matter, she said. *You always will. It feels right to ask.*

I closed the distance between us, wrapping her in my arms. She held me close, turning her head to kiss my cheek.

The sensation of her lips on my skin—of place and scent and her body pressed against mine—flooded me with memories and woke a spark low in my belly. It was only meeting of the minds, but it was real all the same.

She slipped a finger beneath my chin and lifted my lips to hers for a kiss that pushed the boundaries of friendship. For that moment, we shared desire, love, and hope. Then she pulled away, meeting my gaze with a shine in her eyes.

I never thought we'd come back here again, she said.

Me either. Of course, I hadn't bet on returning the first time, charging into the Order to find the End.

Déjà vu, she said.

We do what we have to.

She nodded, bending to kiss me again, this time with finality.

In case you're wondering, that's not goodbye, she said. *That would be shitty. And I'll never tell you goodbye. You're going to live forever.*

I raised a brow.

She looked away. I didn't need to see her face to know she'd allowed too much emotion to the surface.

Time to go, Sanchez. I'm kicking you out.

There was more to say, but we weren't going to say it.

I retreated to my own mind as we reached the bottom of the basement stairs and pushed through the veil of protection.

Stacy had taken charge of the group, waving her arms and snapping orders until everyone assembled, Michael included, formed a circle. She yanked the purple band off her head and twisted it around her wrist, blond curls flying free.

"Join hands," she said. When Michael hesitated, she glared at him. "Or get the fuck out."

To my surprise, he chose door number one, taking Miguel's hand and reaching for mine.

His hand felt warm, as if it burned from the inside. Sunday's was chilled. I gazed across the circle into Red's eyes. He felt far away, as if he'd walled off a part of himself.

I reached through the heart link. He answered right away, setting his sacred heart alight, his halo deep green and a brown so dark, it was almost black. He was rooted in the earth beneath the floor, grounded and centered and solid.

He was the only one. The others hung on tenterhooks of one kind or another, their halos a dance of changeable color and light, sweat popping out on brows and the base of spines.

"Deep breath, people," Stacy said.

We drew in air and exhaled as one.

"Again," she said, over and over until the feel of the room shifted from high and chaotic to low and steady.

She pulled a knife from the pocket of her skirt, flicking it open to slice her palm, cupping her hand to let her blood pool. She licked the blade clean and snapped it shut, returning it to her skirt. Not one movement wasted, not one drop spilled.

She couldn't let it. No accidents, only purposeful action. Her blood, like Beth's, carried Malek's poison.

The last time we'd done this, she'd just become his. She hadn't wanted to use her blood as a part of her magic, but she'd bucked up and done what she had to. It'd worked like a charm.

"If you're worrying that this blood will hurt you, it won't. If you're worried that it will tie you to Malek, it won't. It follows my intention, and I won't let that happen. It ties you to me, and through me to each other. We'll share each others' thoughts and magic, like before. There will be lingering effects like last time. They might last longer. Any questions?"

No one spoke.

She stalked across the circle, halting in front of Michael. She held his gaze for a heartbeat. Her magic licked the edges of her body, spilling over into the air around her, filling the space around us and flowing to encompass the others.

Michael made no move to avoid what was about to happen. Surprised the hell out of me. I'd fully expected him to balk at this, to want to keep his thoughts and magic to himself, to follow his directive from whoever made his rules and get out of here before he could be seen to be actually helping us.

Stacy dipped her finger into the blood, then drew an equal-armed cross on the archangel's forehead and over his heart.

The blood sank into his skin and through the fabric of his T-shirt. It was invisible to the eye, but worked its wonders beneath the surface, opening connections and forging bonds.

Stacy stepped to the left, in front of Miguel.

The archangel leaned close, his voice low. "I'm here because I need the door to Miguel."

"You could've done that some other way," I said.

"True."

As Stacy stepped away from Miguel, the archangel faded from the circle. One moment, he was there. In the next, the boundaries of his body seemed to melt before he vanished entirely.

I shook my head.

Miguel didn't seem fazed. He took my hand. "What are you pissed about?"

"I expected him to stick around for the whole thing."

"You're mad he's gone?"

"I'm not mad, exactly."

"Then what?"

"A door to you constructed this way is a door to the rest of us," I said.

"Think he'll try to do something we haven't agreed to?"

"Meddle? Stick his nose where it doesn't belong and try to control us?"

Miguel laughed.

It wasn't funny. "If you were him?"

Miguel sighed.

After that, there was nothing to do but wait until Stacy came full circle, stopping in front of me. The depths of her eyes were the color of her indigo halo, and unreadable.

"May the powers protect you if they can," she said. "May they have your back and back your play."

Her words echoed in my heart and mind as she marked them with the last of the blood in her cupped palm. My mind filled with a cacophony of voices, each with its own distinct flavor and sound and trace of magic.

Two voices stood out above the din.

La Muerte whispered in my mind, mapping the path forward from here. Telling me tales about the End.

The End wasn't a Horseman. He wasn't an angel or a demon or fae.

He was a force. He could hive off his consciousness to hijack unwilling humans. He could control them with his malevolent will. He was many times larger than *La Muerte*, so he couldn't fold all of himself into one human vessel. But he could get damn close.

It seemed clear now that he'd chosen Mark for that reason. Mark still had miles left in him. He could still be used, ridden, discarded.

Our world was everything the End hated. It would weaken him. He could not survive in this world in his original form. He'd found a place to use as his home base. Somewhere secret that couldn't be traced on any map, one that couldn't be guessed. Ideally, it would be mobile, ever-changing—or a place where no one would think to look. A place that held magic in its bones, where doors opened into other realms.

I thought of all the places where Mark and the End could've gone to ground. If it were me, I'd have built my fortress next-door to every realm. Easy access. Easy escape.

My building something there might screw with the physics of the place, making it less desirable as a go-to road between the worlds.

Jesus.

The second voice coming in with clarity and strength, painted with an East Texas drawl. Red.

He spoke a single word, over and over. My name.

That sound and the love it carried were everything. I held tight to it, and felt his sacred heart ignite before I glimpsed the glow behind the fabric of his shirt. The fire in my own heart answered.

I know where the End is, I said.

So do the rest of us.

That was how this spell worked, this connection.

Beth intruded, her mind's voice knocking at our door. *Famine is near the river.*

Which one? I asked.

The Willamette. There's a black fog there, Night. It feels empty, like it's drawing in all the air around it. Like a black hole.

Can you go there now? Go ahead, sniff around?

I'm the bait, she said. *No problem.*

I sent her love because she needed it, and because I felt it, whole and complete.

Love was here, inside this house with Red. With my family. I might leave the house, leave them. But they would never leave me. I needed to know that in my marrow, to feel sure of it and hold on to it.

Out there—where we were going—there was only war.

CHAPTER 13

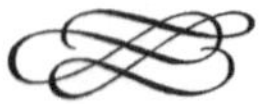

S HADOWS SLICKED the wide stretch of the Willamette River, shrouding the water in darkness. The lights of buildings and bridges should've reflected in on its surface, but tonight the river felt disconnected from its surroundings, as if it existed in a different realm. Even the starlight couldn't touch it, no matter the frigid clarity of the air without so much as a wisp of cloud. I tasted nothing on the air—not snow, not the water, not the crushed grass of the west waterfront beneath my feet. Stray cars and semis raced along ribbons of concrete, but the white-noise-dull-roar of their passage didn't reach me.

Something—or someone—had carved a place for themselves right here at the foot of the Hawthorne Bridge. Every sound and smell and taste that flowed in, every light and every evidence of life, vanished here. Taken. Used. Destroyed.

The east wind blasted strong enough to break my balance, carrying frost in its fists and whipping the tendrils of hair that escaped from my braid into my narrowed eyes. The darkest space, not only void of light, but seemingly void of air and life, hovered over a brick circle on the sidewalk. The red star that filled the circle was gone, swallowed by the darkness.

I knew what the dark was about because the Angel knew. Walking into that void meant walking into destruction. It meant undoing everything you were. If you managed to walk out again, you would be utterly changed.

Only a fool would do such a thing.

I felt Sunday, circling around to the left. I saw through her eyes, clear and unblinking, her rose-gold halo flaring like the sun. I felt Miguel, circling around on the right, his usual bruised halo replaced with the blaze of the archangel Michael's, his eyes full of fire. He wore Michael's denim and black and his magic bent the air around him.

We got this, he said.

I prayed we did, that our plan gave us the advantage of surprise we hoped for.

"We got this," I said, and stepped from the grass onto the walk. One step closer to the dark.

A surge of power erupted under me. I braced myself, but the blast of magic wasn't meant to hurt me. It settled into a scraping, crushing tension, like the crash of one iceberg into another. The temperature dropped ten degrees. The air stung my lungs. My wings strained inside my backpack. They wanted to be free.

I slipped out of the pack, keeping my wings folded because of the wind. I couldn't care whether anyone saw me at this point, or whether they realized that I wasn't in costume and that this wasn't a *Keep Portland Weird* moment. Any innocent bystander who didn't run might end up dead, but I couldn't do much to help that. Not anymore. Not here.

A human silhouette separated itself from the circle's edge, moving toward me, its halo resolving to bright orange threaded with black. No innocent bystander, but Beth.

Beth's eyes were wild behind her black-framed glasses, her braids writhing in the wind like Medusa's hair. She pressed her mouth into a thin line, curling her hands into fists and shaking them out.

"Do you feel that?" she asked.

I nodded.

"How did he gain a foothold in this world? How did we let him do this?"

There were too many fights. We couldn't be everywhere at once. We'd focused on what landed in front of us, always reacting, never searching out a battle. The crises came so fast and hard that we never had a chance to glimpse the big picture, only the smaller pieces of the puzzle. And that would never change because we were human, or close enough to human that our extra senses or powers couldn't make up the difference.

"We can't think far enough into the future," I said. "We can't think far enough in the past. If we were going up against other human beings, we'd be all right. But the beings we're fighting are older than time and they're going to live forever. They're playing a longer game. Our time is finite. Theirs is infinite."

"You are them, Night."

"Not yet."

"We're screwed." She closed the distance between us, hugging herself against the cold. "Have you seen yourself? You look like a… well, you look like shit. You're turning, Night. Whatever's going to happen for you and the Angel, it's starting for real."

"I know," I said.

Because I was turning, I could see more deeply into the stronghold the End had built. Yes, it appeared to be empty of heat and light and heart on the outside, but beyond that it tasted like a puzzle. Like a maze. Like a trap that would hold anyone stupid enough to enter without a map.

I could see and taste those things because they promised death.

I read a million questions on her face, but she didn't ask them.

Would I be able to hold up through this fight? Would my body or my mind or my souls collapse as the Angel and I were remade? Would my magic fail? Would his? What would happen in that moment?

I held her gaze. "If Malek hadn't ordered you to come, would you still have done it? If you didn't owe me, would you be here?"

She cocked her head. "Why ask me now?"

"Is there a better time?"

"I guess not," she said. "If you or one of the others had called me? I'd have come."

"You wanted to stay home. You wanted time off."

She shrugged. "I still like to pretend I have a normal life sometimes."

My mouth quirked. "Don't we all?"

I felt the presence of another Horseman. The familiarity, the gravity, the power. Famine's magic, aimed and ready. Mine rose to meet it.

"Beth?"

"I know. She's here."

We turned to meet Famine's dark saucer gaze behind the shiny lenses of her tortoiseshell glasses. Her pigtails and the hem of her navy dress whipped in the wind. As I watched, she grew a foot taller and wider.

Beth set her hands on her hips. "Hey, girl."

Famine laughed, the sound echoing off the brick. "I never tire of playing with you, Beth, but I'm not here for you tonight. This is your chance to leave if you want to live. You should take it."

Beth shook her head. "Nah."

I glanced from Famine to Beth and back again.

There was something between the two of them—more than the Famine's desire to murder Beth once and for all. Rivalry? A desperate desire to understand the other? Some kind of twisted sisterhood?

Famine raised a brow, looking past Beth to pin me with her gaze. "You can come with me, Night. I'll take you to him. You can see for yourself that he's not the enemy. He's our father."

Beth's turn to laugh. "Wait—you think she came here to give herself up? Night Sanchez, Angel of Death, on your side?"

"Yes," Famine said.

The Angel's power rose in me, woven with my magic. He looked through my eyes, heard with my ears, felt the wind as it raced over my skin. His consciousness melded with mine. He experienced the small slice of the world in which we stood as I did.

I felt the beginnings of time in his power, the march of millennia and the turn of ages. I saw the world through his eyes—the empty waterfront filled with forms that my magic hadn't been able to register, pale wisps of spirit that clung to the world after they should've moved on.

Ghosts. The riverbank was awash with the spirits of the dead.

The wind blew through them, the gusts affecting them not at all. Why were they here?

They're not ours, the Angel said.

We were cold. We were ice.

Our warp and weft connected, sealing the bond that had begun the moment I'd taken the Angel into my mind to save Faith, from the moment he'd matched magic and wits with me and fallen to my will. The last vestiges of me, Night, as a single, finite, solitary human being with my own thoughts and feelings and ambitions and free will, vanished in that moment, as did his.

We became a breath in the storm, a silent, still moment.

The change that had begun would accelerate from here. It would take us both down, but not this moment. Not now. We needed to hold on a little longer.

The magic and the will I'd used to strengthen my physical body still held. The Angel fed what power he could into that spell, buying us time. Would it be enough?

All of them—Sunday, Miguel, and Faith and everyone else connected by the blood link that Stacy had forged—felt the change. One by one, as understanding overcame them, I felt what they did: shock, sorrow, grief.

The strength of it threatened to take me to my knees.

I held onto hope.

I didn't know whether I could go home from here, or whether they would take me in if I tried. My heart cracked open, bleeding and raw. Home felt far away. I didn't have time to grieve it. I only had time to love.

My love was powerful. My love was fierce.

Magic beat within my heart and spilled over my skin, coating my wings. It dripped from my fingertips. It flowed from my eyes and infused my voice. It branded every part of me, burning itself into my being. It was there to stay, always.

Famine's eyes widened. After a moment, she smiled.

"Welcome home," she said, magic flowing through her words.

It washed over me like warm water, stinging against my chilled skin and cold magic, tasting of promises and lies, of hopes and dreams not yet realized, of hunger so deep that it could never be sated, of thirst so bottomless, it could never be filled.

I could have it all if I followed her. My apocalyptic destiny, all the power the Angel of Death wielded and more, once the fourth Horseman was found and accepted their fate. My humanity, the tender parts of myself, vulnerable and flawed and afraid. The love I'd found with Red. The family we'd become with Faith and Corey and Sunday, with Addie and Jess and Ben. All I would have to do to make them mine the way I wanted them—the way I needed them—was kill them.

I cocked my head at Famine, holding her saucer gaze with my own. She really thought she could overtake my will. She thought she could trap me in a spell. Use my hunger against me.

She thought that if she took me down—me, Night—that the Angel would take over. She thought that had been the Angel's plan all along.

Beth took a wide step away—not from Famine, but from me. I glanced over my shoulder in time to see Faith, Sunday, and Miguel do the same.

I drew a sharp breath. Famine hadn't been trying to overpower me at all. She'd simply reached into me and activated the blood link that Stacy had built, shooting her magic through the connections between me and the others like a dozen arrows that struck home and anchored in my family's oldest, most instinctive drive—their hunger to survive.

Whether the Angel took me was immaterial. If she could make my people believe he had, if she could make them believe we would kill them, she could turn them into a weapon against me.

I reached for Stacy, feeling the open channel of magic between us begin to close, hearing the words she chanted miles away in the chilled basement of Addie's house, shutting the way between us to protect herself—whether from Famine's magic or from me made no difference.

Stacy was cutting me off. Breaking the one magical joining we needed to go up against the End and have any hope of emerging on the other side of the fight.

Five seconds at most before the flow of power between us died. Four. Three.

Maintaining the connection in the face of opposition would cost us. It might cost us everything.

We fired our magic through the channel, rocketing all the way in before Stacy choked it off, invading her mind, battling her will and a surge of animal terror that crashed over her. I wrested control of her and connected with Addie's magic and Jess's, with Ben's and Corey's, with Faith's and Sunday's and Miguel's.

The Angel and I steamrolled over objections and wards and any other boundaries they'd set to protect their magic from being stolen. We wrested their power—all of it. Ben's shield, we deployed as magical armor in front of my friends and my daughter where they stood. With the rest, we took aim at the darkness the End had built.

We blasted the gathered magic at the dark, striking a blow with the combined magic we'd used once before to hurt the End, to force him back.

The power descended, shattering the dark into countless feathers of darkness that whirled in the wind, then fell to the ground, staining the snow and grass and concrete before they faded away, leaving the entrance to the End's stronghold exposed.

No more maze to trap the unwary.

Where the red star should've been, a hole in the ground gaped, its maw bigger than three of me, wingspan included. It looked deep and dark and my imagination painted sharp teeth on every side, ready to spear me bloody if I tried to pass.

The Angel's words echoed in my heart. *We can see in the dark.*

There will be more snares down there. More places prepared to trap us.

No, the Angel said. *The snares are for your family. He wants you to find him. Alone.*

I'm never alone.

We let go of my family's magic, drawing back into our shifting, changing body.

As we did, Beth launched herself at Famine, tackling the Horseman in a tangle of arms and legs and gnashing teeth, the Horseman trying —and failing—to open portal after portal. To remove Beth from the battlefield.

Sunday roared in from behind them, gaze locked on me, hands curled into fists so tight, her nails sliced her palms. Her blood dripped onto the patch of snow where she stood. She looked at me as if I were her destination. Not friend. Not enemy. The thin set of her mouth was all raw determination. Then she glanced past me to the spirits at the water's edge.

"They're coming," she said.

Miguel moved in beside her, his halo like the sun, eyes filled with fire, jaw clenched. "Then we stop them."

I ran for the open hole in the ground—the door that led to the End —and dove in, wings catching air as they snapped wide.

The darkness swallowed me. My eyes adjusted quickly, picking up variations in shadow and pinpoints of gray, but no actual light. No teeth menaced from the sides of the hole. It was made from earth all around, its surface burnt—cauterized, like a wound, to stop the bleeding. It stank of fire and tasted of death. Charred earthworms and insects, dampness boiled dry.

The air grew colder—well below freezing. Ice began to crystallize on my lashes. I could neither see nor feel the bottom. The passage might go on forever. I might fall forever. The bottom dropped out of my heart, the weight of it punching down into the bowl of my belly like a fist.

Right on cue, a heavy, grunting weight struck my back, hands clawing for purchase. I leveled out slightly to give Faith a second to grab hold—arms around my shoulders with fingers clasped at my throat, legs wrapped around my waist.

I could feel her physically. I couldn't feel her magically, not even this close, with her hands on me. Ben had shielded her well. And Stacy had sent her to me exactly as planned, from the basement to this place and time.

That they'd gone through with it after what Famine had tried— after I'd forced the connection to remain open and hijacked their magic—

"Are they okay?" I asked.

"Yes," Faith said.

If I couldn't sense her power, then odds were that the End couldn't either. She was our surprise. Our hope.

The temperature dropped again, the mist of my breath freezing a rime on my lips. The icy air seeping through our clothes and skin, into our flesh and blood and bone. It made no difference to the Angel and me, but Faith began to shiver.

I spoke to her through the blood link. *Use your magic to warm you.*

She shook her head. *My magic blows things up.*

That's all you've used it for so far. Your magic is the source of all magic. Ask the god within for help.

She was silent for a long moment, taking that in and then using it as a stick to beat herself up. She should've known to do that. She should've figured it out herself. Then she forced those thoughts underground and got down to business.

She could do recriminations later. Right now, there was only the threat of her freezing to death before she could help me.

Her mind and heart blazed with the silver and gold of her halo. The light broke into streams of color, some shadowed and some bright, creating images that made no sense to me but meant everything to Faith. The Awakened answered her, shaking the silver and gold into glittering sand and reshaping it into pictures to convey its response.

Faith stopped shivering. The Awakened supplemented the natural heat of her body and halo, raising her temperature to combat the cold inside and out.

Think and look outside the box, I said. *Don't be afraid of what you find.*

She nodded. *How much farther? Can you see the bottom?*

I couldn't. We'd been falling for a long time.

The sides of the hole looked exactly the same as they had at first—like charred earth. They smelled of the same burnt death.

And the barest hint of sulfur.

Sulfur meant the In-Between, and the In-Between meant portals. We'd been falling through portals that led powers-knew-where. Portals designed to take us further away from the End—or to lead us to him in a way that made it impossible for our friends to follow.

Or to distract us. To keep us busy long enough for the End to do —what?

Mom? Something's happening at the house. Corey's freaking out. Can you feel it?

I honed my attention through the blood link, catching a low-level panic that hadn't yet risen to full-steam before I slipped into Corey's consciousness.

She stood in the center of the basement, rug red as blood beneath her feet. The skull cameos at her throat and ears and on her fingers flashed the same bone white as her halo. She could barely see through the light she created.

Her arms hung straight at her sides, fingers splayed, as human shapes rose through the floor in front of her, taking on solid form as they entered the space. Hair, eyes, clothes reminiscent of who they'd once been. Frost flowed from their skin, icing every surface they touched.

The killing cold of the End.

CHAPTER 14

PORTALS! *Look for edges and energy shifts. Do it now!*
I shot the words into Faith's mind with enough force to tear her focus from Corey. Faith snarled at me.

I need to help her—

No. I'll do it. I'll be flying blind for a minute. I need you.

She snapped her mental mouth shut. Charred earth surrounded us and icy air roared in our ears—the fall went on and on, with no sign of the bottom. Powers only knew where we were, or what was happening to our people at the waterfront.

Our people at the house were under attack.

Faith sent the Awakened images, and he sent pictures back. They had magic. They *were* magic. They would use it only if they needed to. Stay hidden unless there was no other choice. I had to trust them as they trusted me.

The Angel and I left as much of consciousness as we could in charge of flight and body mechanics, rocketing the rest of our awareness to Corey.

Ben stood beside her, long bangs in his eyes, painstakingly building a stone-gray shield around the two of them. Would it hold against the spirits of the dead? Maybe against spirits without a malevolent hand directing their every move. Against spirits controlled by the End?

They didn't stand a chance.

The End and Famine had coordinated this attack. It had to be the one they'd planned to use against us if I'd remained in the house. Wait for the Angel and I to go down. Hit us at our most vulnerable.

They'd repurposed, reworked. Used it in the moment Famine had convinced my people that I'd turned on them. The moment I'd wrenched away their magic to use in the field.

Smart. Impossible to defend against.

Stacy had already gone down, and I hadn't felt it. I didn't know how or why, only that she lay unconscious beside Red, skin shaded from its normal pale tone toward blue. Her chest rose and fell, but she was so cold, vapor rose from her body.

Red laid hands on her, the sacred heart on his chest shining so bright, it looked as if it were on fire. The grass and earth of his magic filled the whole room. Heat flowed from his palms. Would it be enough?

The spirits had targeted Stacy strategically. She held open the escape portal. She commanded the magic that connected us all. Her spells would hold without her awake and aware to defend them—as long as they weren't attacked and dismantled by someone with more power.

Red felt the brush of my thoughts against his and my quick tug on the heart link.

Where are you? he asked.

I showed him, a quick flash of where and when and with whom.

Jesus, Night. Go back. We got this.

They didn't have this. They were fucked.

We'll find a way, he said.

Where are Addie and Jess?

Top of the stairs.

Helping the house spirit defend the place. Fighting a lost battle.

I shouted Corey's name, forcing her to turn her attention toward the sound of my voice. The Angel's voice. We felt her eyes widen, her breath come shallow and fast, the cold sweat slick her forehead.

She'd fought before. She'd been present for every battle we'd had since the Angel came to town. This time, only she had the magic to take on the menace. But she used her magic to see and talk with the dead, not to push them away or harm them.

A voice that sounded like Faith's murmured in the back of my consciousness.

(Mom)

Wait, I told her.

Confusion swarmed Corey's mind. *Night? Is that you? You don't sound like yourself. You sound like—*

The Angel, I said.

The last time we'd used the connective magic, everyone had funneled their power toward the people who'd traveled into harm's way. Those who'd remained behind risked attack, but they'd remained safe.

We'd needed them. The power flowed one way, and it'd been enough. Now, they needed us.

(Mom!)

I pushed back. I needed only seconds.

The Angel followed my lead. Instead of taking, we gave.

We sent our magic through the blood link, slipping and sliding into Corey's mind like a drop of ink in clear water, clouding and spreading, adding our power to hers.

She could survive the spirits' deadly touch now, and she could pass the Angel's power through the link to the others. She could use it to wrest control of the dead.

The dead belonged to the Angel.

Corey took a deep breath, planted her feet on the floor with more strength than she felt. She drew her magic up from the base of her spine.

(Mom, now!)

I released my hold on Corey's mind with a prayer for her fight—for Ben's and Addie's and Jess's and oh, God, Red's—

My consciousness slammed back into my winged-flying-Faith's-weight-on-my-back body. My heartbeat rang like a bell, vibrating my cells from the inside out.

One racing heartbeat for my eyes to focus, for horror to take root in my gut, for my training and instinct to steal in, to take over—as we speared through a portal into a stench of sulfur so overwhelming that I choked. Low clouds pressed against snow- and ice-packed earth—rising toward me at blinding speed.

No time to slow. No time to stop.

I snapped my wings close to my body, knocking Faith from her perch, and flipped over just in time to pull her tight. I thrust my wings out again, wrapping them around us, urging them to connect, to form a seal around us.

The feathers hardened from their roots at my back, turning to stone inch by inch.

Not fast enough.

CHAPTER 15

W E HIT THE GROUND like a bomb. Faith exploded from my arms, fire flying from her fingertips. The impact ripped the breath from my body, the shockwave shaking me to the core. I blacked out for a fraction of a second. In that space, the ice beneath me began to crystallize on my clothes, seeping through to burn my skin. My lashes frosted. When I could finally suck in air, the exhalation fogged, turned solid, and fell to the ground like frozen tears.

I rolled over, feathers shedding the stone, and crouched at the ready. My gaze locked on Faith, a splash of silver and gold against the white and gray of this place. She looked small and lost in front of the form the End had taken. Then the magic she'd hidden began to rise within her, the glow of the Awakened's fire igniting at her fingertips.

Mark looked exactly the same as he had in Addie's basement, beard and green knit cap with matching coat, brown hikers on his feet. A black hole of a halo. The lines around his mouth had deepened into canyons, their track spreading across the sides of his face all the way to his ears. The sunken shadows under his eyes and the dead white of his skin made him look like a corpse.

He wasn't dead—yet. But he was damn close. The End had just about iced the humanity out of him. He'd left his apartment one morning to pick up his partner at the airport and he would die today, either by my hand or from housing the unimaginable power of the End.

His hands trembled, the motion so slight that I'd have missed it if I hadn't been looking for some sign of humanity in him, some part of him I could influence or control, use to our advantage.

Faith needed a minute to detonate a charge big enough to hurt the End. She wasn't going to get it.

Back away, I said. *One touch from him is all it will take. He'll turn you to ice.*

He reached for her.

The Angel and I sent our magic through the blood link, shielding her as Mark's hand closed over her shoulder, fingernails digging in.

Mark's voice sounded rusty, as if he didn't know how to use it—or so much power poured through him, his vocal cords were breaking down.

"This is who all the fuss has been about? The god within you is nothing. You can't hurt me. You can't save your mother. You can't even save yourself."

Faith couldn't move. It wasn't the End's magic that transfixed her, but what he'd said. She stared at him.

"You might be the one—someday," he said. "But not yet."

She grabbed his hand to burn him, to pull it away, but he was stronger.

He dragged her off her feet with that one hand and tossed her aside as if she were made of moss and sticks instead of human parts. As he threw her, the Angel and I shoved our magic into Mark's mind, searching for signs that some part of Mark was awake and aware, trying to resist the End.

We pummeled through defenses that should have been stronger, tumbling into a hall of mirrors created from shards of ice, smooth and polished as glass. Every surface reflected my face, the rich brown of my skin bleached nearly white, the edges of my dark pupils burning with white fire.

Mark was nowhere to be found.

Another trap. Another snare set to take advantage of who I was, my skillset, my magic. Me—Night—not the Angel of Death. I'd led us in because that was what I always did, because it always worked. Invading, finding the right fear, the most desperate hope, gaining control—that was how I killed. That was what I knew.

Everything I'd been trained to do, everything I knew, was wrong.

How could I gain control of the End when he'd shattered himself into pieces and placed those parts in unsuspecting humans roaming my city—and powers only knew where else? Even with a majority of himself stuffed into the man in front of me, the best I could do was to kill the man. End Mark's life.

The End would just find another like him, and another. He'd run through them as if they were disposable. To him, they were.

Ice glittered all around. The walls began to close in. I glanced back the way I'd come. The hole in the End's defenses we'd smashed? Gone. No path out remained.

The mirrors might be a trap, but they were no illusion. To my magic and my mind, they were real. They could crush the life out of me. They could imprison me, just like I'd jailed the Angel in my mind at the start.

The reflection in the ice shifted. I stared. I couldn't stop. I could barely breathe.

The image of my face faded, replaced by the shine of city lights on the surface of the Willamette River, the waterfront a patchwork of snow-dusted grass, concrete, and brick. The hole Faith and I'd dived into gaped like a hungry mouth. At its edge, my team fought with all the magic they had.

A jade blade, gilded sigils carved into its surface, glinted in Beth's hand. The poison of Beth's blood infected its edge. If she could scratch Famine with it, the Horseman would go down—or retreat. Either served our purpose. Either would save lives.

But Beth hadn't landed a single blow. Famine looked as strong as ever, and Beth bled from a dozen cuts. She taunted the Horseman.

I heard what Beth said—it poured into me through the blood link.

What makes you think you can win? You've lost every fight with me. You can't kill me—not permanently. You can't stop me.

But it was just Beth against Famine. Sunday and Miguel couldn't help her. They faced off against the line of spirits that had gathered at the waterline. Spirits like those at the house, animated by the End, set against them.

Sunday blinded them. Miguel blasted them with borrowed archangel's fire. The spirits more than fell before the onslaught—they vaporized, their souls burned to cinders. They ceased to exist utterly.

They were innocents, just like any other being the End had taken over. Their human lives were over, but they were alive all the same. What Sunday and Miguel did to them—what they had no choice but to do—meant a true death for those spirits. No afterlife. No reunion with loved ones.

Sunday operated on training and instinct. Do or die. Kill or be killed. Recriminations were for later.

Miguel deployed Michael's fire with shaking hands. His chameleon magic tasted the spirits' lives. The way this woman's granddaughter laughed, and how that laughter was the sound of pure joy. That man's loneliness, so deeply embedded in the heart that even when others reached out, he couldn't reach back.

These were their lived memories. He destroyed them, and the spirits along with them.

He and Sunday would go on destroying whatever they had to in order to survive. In order to give us a chance.

If the reflections in the ice showed the truth, the fight at the river had come to a fragile stalemate. If Famine killed Beth—only a matter of time—then Famine would descend on Sunday and Miguel, pinning them between the spirits of the dead and a Horseman of the Apocalypse. They were good, but not that good.

The End had sprung trap after trap.

The reflections in the ice shifted again, this time to show me the snow-covered ground on which I stood in the In-Between, Mark possessed in front of me and Faith thrown to my right.

A different kind of ice settled in the bowl of my belly.

I reached for Faith through the blood link, fighting the interference from the trap, barely touching her muddy mind, barely feeling the suffocating sensation of her lungs gulping sulfur-stained air, unable to get enough.

Alive for now, but for how long?

Or the mirror lied to me, like every other trap the End had set.

The Angel's voice—my voice, our voice—burst through all doubt, bringing the hammer down with a sound that shook every sheet of ice around me, shook me to the bone.

No.

Faith's image vanished from the ice. I stared at my own reflection. Just mine. And the Angel's. He was there in the wings folded along my back, black feathers and bone and muscle, in the star fire that rimmed my pupils, in the grave-chill that frosted my brown skin.

The hall of mirrors held me, no exit in sight. The reflections had appeared at exactly the moment I'd realized the snare had closed, distracting me from finding or forcing a way out. While I'd been enthralled, the hall had tightened its grip further. Now, in addition to mirrors for walls, the reflecting surface extended to above and below, ahead and behind.

Attempting to break out using magic carried a high risk that anything the Angel and I sent into the mirrors would return to me with the same—or magnified—power.

I was out of my depth. The End, out of my league.

That had been true before, back in the hall of angels at the Order. In the battle to free the magical children on whom the End fed, we'd needed everyone's magic, woven with mine and *La Muerte*'s, to strike a single blow. We'd won the day. We'd saved a handful of kids. It'd been worth it, and I'd do it all again in a heartbeat.

But this time was different, because the End had become more than a single being we needed to work together to defeat.

Like the other Elders or other beings of that stature—Dream, Shadow, Michael—the End couldn't be killed. He could only be pushed back, remaining to fight another day.

The End, if he'd ever been a single being coalesced into one codified form, had become something else. By splintering his consciousness and invading who knew how many humans, he'd made himself a part of humanity.

He couldn't have done that in only the last few weeks. Building this place in the In-Between alone would've taken longer. Like I'd said to Beth, humans couldn't wrap their minds around the length and breadth of planning the End was capable of. And this was the Apocalypse, a battle foretold millennia ago.

The End had been building this stronghold forever. He'd been piecing himself out forever, too. Making humanity his own.

What was this one battle against all of that? What could we possibly do to turn the tide?

I could feel the sustaining magic begin to fade, its edges chipping away, cracks at its center, holding on by a hair. Any moment now, those cracks would spread and the spell would crumble. I would no longer be able to stand. To fight. Not until the transformation was over.

That would happen without any kind of push, or any action at all, from the Angel and me. Maybe we could blast open the trap, rebound risk or not, but chances were we didn't have more than one shot at it.

The Angel was willing.

I knew better. I needed to stop thinking about the big picture and consider the small one: the hall of mirrors.

I was a master of mind magic. I killed by exploiting fears. I couldn't get to Mark's mind. Mark's mind was nothing at all, here and now.

The Angel was a master of death, of body and soul.

He didn't ask whether I was sure. He didn't note that, since escaping from the Order, I hadn't killed a single person who didn't deserve it—operatives sent after me and rogue Watchers, but not innocent bystanders caught up in a cosmic game. He didn't mourn for the life Mark had once had, or the people who loved him and whom he loved, or for all the things he would never have the chance to do.

I did, the emotion condensed into the space of a heartbeat. I shouldered it. Took responsibility for it. Made a place for Mark's soul within my heart.

Killing Mark will break the trap, the Angel said. *It will break us. It will not break the End.*

I saw it clearly, as *La Muerte* saw it. The part of the End housed within Mark would seek out the nearest possible vessel—Faith or me. Faith and the god within her would fight this. We would not be able to.

The humanity within me would be busy dying. That was what it came down to. Dying to become Death. The last piece of the puzzle. My last human act.

The End would take advantage of that. It would invade. The Angel and I wouldn't have the strength to fight it off. Not on our own.

I took a deep breath, feeling the weight of my physical body, the firing of synapses, the rush of blood, the beating of my heart, the fire low in my belly. In a moment, it would all be lost. I could hope that it would return, but it would never be the same.

I sent love through the heart link to Red, and felt him answer—strength, courage, love. Whatever I needed him to hold for me, to send to me, he would.

I closed my eyes, the last punch of woven magic rising, wild with raw power and cold. So cold.

CHAPTER 16

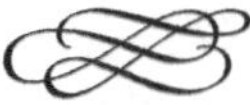

T HE ANGEL'S MAGIC, irrevocably woven with mine, did not blast forth. It crept from us like a predator stalking the shadows, shapeshifting to match the End's ice, melding with it, sinking through the hall of mirrors. It followed the paths the End had laid within Mark's body, the framework of magic that supported his presence within Mark, coming home to the place where magic began and ended: the heart.

Our magic was a finger to the heart, a choice to take his life.

The End screamed, the sound shattering the mirrors, exploding ice shards all around us. They arrowed for our eyes, our mouth, our veins.

The Angel's power stopped them at the edges of our halo. They fell at our feet, the magic drained from them.

There was nothing the End could do. He could fight this, but he would lose. This was our destiny. Our sacred task, and no one, not even the architect of the end of all worlds, would keep us from it.

Mark dropped where he stood.

The trap sprung, our magic shot back into my body, into living flesh and blood and bone on the verge of giving up the ghost. The strengthening spell gave way, the last vestiges of it washing away as the wave of change rose within us. For a heartbeat, it paused at the top of its arc, animation suspended, its weight held back by love and will.

My legs refused to hold me. I went down, first to my knees, and then over on my side. As I fell, Faith turned her head toward me, opening her eyes in time to see me hit the snow with a thud that shook me to the core.

She blinked at me, taking in what was happening, listening to the god inside her, aware of all movement, all possibilities.

I spoke to her through the blood link. *I'm sorry.*

I said it even though I'd done what I could for her and for all of them—what needed to be done. I didn't want to leave her. I didn't want her to see this.

It's okay, she said. *We're gonna take care of this now.*

I tried to shake my head, but the muscles refused to obey.

Let go, she said. *It's all right to let go.*

As if my heart needed her permission, my body began to shut down. My vision fuzzed until I could no longer make out lines and curves, only colors. The feeling in my hands and feet left, and the numbness spiraled up my arms and legs. Cold overtook my center, darkening the light in the pit of my belly, working its way around and up my back, swallowing the crown of my head and dimming the star fire in my eyes. It stole my voice and my breath, traveling swiftly toward my heart.

The link I shared with Red flared, red and gold and full of life. I felt him holding on as if he were right here in the sulfured snow, his warmth bleeding into my chill, his heartbeat steady and strong. And. Right. Here.

The love and will that held the wave at bay began to falter. The magic crashed over the Angel and me, drowning out dreams and wishes and desperation.

The heart link died an agonizing second before my heart stopped.

Time took a deep breath and blew it out slowly. The world froze—a gust of wind in mid-passage, the blink of Faith's lashes at half-mast, the pouring of the End's life force from Mark's nose and mouth, from the pores of his skin, halfway to my body.

I shouldn't be able to see at all, but the colors hadn't left me: Faith's silver-and-gold sweater, her black hair and dark eyes, the silver of my hourglass pendant at her throat; the white of the snow and the yellow staining the air; the roiled cloud of nothingness suspended between Mark and me. Shapes began to return. Then sound—the sound of silence so loud, it filled my head with pressure.

My heart beat once. It felt as if its movement and rhythm might crack open my chest.

Twice. Blood surged through my body.

Three times. I sucked in air.

Time shot into motion again. Faith pushed to her feet. The roiling cloud—the End—billowed and slammed into me where I lay.

I tried to move again, but my muscles weren't yet ready. I could only lie there while the End infiltrated my skin, while his empty cloud poured down my throat and up my nose, tasting of smoke and ashes.

I closed my eyes, the better to see within, the better to mark the End's passage through my body. He built paths as he wended his way toward my heart.

Our heart, the Angel said.

Yes, it was. We would not let the End take it without a fight.

CHAPTER 17

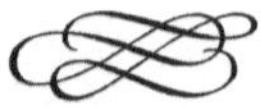

THE END WRAPPED his life force around our heart, a fist seeking to crush, to destroy. To make our home his own. His power against ours. He had total control. We could barely use what we had.

The snow beneath us clung to me, the End's ice seeping in with a cold so deep, it burned. My breath came shallow and quick. The sulfured air and the darkness seemed to close in, swallowing the space around us, hugging the edges of my body. Claustrophobia exploded under the surface of our skin, and fight or flight kicked in hard and fast—only our body still refused the order to move, so we could do neither.

The Angel's wings—those beside our heart—turned to smoke, from feathers we could feel to something more ephemeral, reshaping into something sharper. Talons that tore at the End, slicing through its black-hole being.

With every strike, every blow that ripped him apart, the End reconstituted himself, healing, covering, crafting better defenses.

Scrabbling to my right warned me to look out again just in time to glimpse Faith sliding toward me, sparks from her fingertips melting the snow in her wake. She skidded to a halt beside us, rolling us over onto our back with a grunt and planting her hands on our chest as if she could drive out the End like that.

If she detonated her magic, she'd hurt the Angel and me—not the End.

She met our gaze. That wasn't her intent at all.

Instead of a blast of pure magical fire, she sent a tendril of flame that snaked through our skin, lighting up the Angel's talons with her power, forcing the End to turn away from the heart to face the threat.

That gave the Angel and me enough of an edge to keep from going under—more than that, it allowed us to climb on top of the fight, to give our body a chance to recover, our magic a chance to spread its wings.

Hold on, Mom.

Her voice rang inside our head, its clarity edged with static. The link between us still held, but something had shifted in my blood with the change.

We felt her reach for the others. Those who could answer did so, one by one. They saw our battle through her eyes. They filled her with their magic and she sent it through our physical connection.

Addie's and Jess's Watcher power sinking into the End, unmaking everything he built, tearing it apart piece by piece.

Ben's shield, surrounding me, fortifying us from the inside out.

An effort to keep the End locked inside. To imprison him in our body.

The hell was going on?

Can you hold tight? Faith asked. *All of you?*

Every single one of them sent an affirmation.

Faith looked into our eyes, her magic beginning to wind its way around our body, heading for the spot where the wings emerged. Threads of silver and gold flame rolled through muscle and bone, from roots to feathered tips.

I need you to fly, she said. *Can you do that?*

With the fight going on inside, with the change not yet complete, it would take every ounce of energy, every particle of will, to make that happen.

Where? we asked.

Where you came from, she said. *To the waterfront, to Sunday and Beth and Miguel.*

And Famine and the army of spirits the End commanded.

What's the plan?

Don't worry about that. Go with it.

We didn't have the wherewithal to argue. The choice was simple: do or don't.

Do or die, she said.

If you remove your hands, will the collective magic remain with us?

I don't know.

We took a deep breath, leveraging our wings to sit. That small action raised a film of sweat on our brow. The flight from the In-Between would be much worse. If our wings failed mid-flight, if we fell—if that happened, we would be seriously hurt. Faith might get worse. If we encountered another trap the End had laid, we could become caught in it. We could—

Anything could happen. But not if *La Muerte* and I stayed here, hesitating from fear.

We pushed to our feet, Faith's hands falling away. The bolstering magic began to fall away. Addie's and Jess's faded first, then Faith's. Ben's stone shield crumbled to dust.

The End cried victory. Alone, the Angel and I had no chance to keep him at bay, not yet. His fist closed around our heart, the threads of his power sliding in, weaving a black hole web of darkness. He leached the new life from the blood and muscle. Forced the rhythm of our heartbeat to shift, to make room for him to abide there.

Nothing the Angel or I did stopped him or even gave him pause. Not the talons of our magic. Not the power of our will.

Rage roared in our belly. Hate crawled across our skin. Despair bloomed in our chest.

Another moment and we would belong to him, his power lifting and changing and co-opting our magic.

When that happened, the sky was the limit. We weren't Mark or any of the other humans whose lives he'd stolen. We were a cosmic force all our own, one he could use to his own ends without giving orders, without negotiation.

We would become more than a sign of the Apocalypse. We would become the end of the world. We could kill hundreds, thousands, millions. Not just humans, but other beings as well, in all the realms. We could kill the worlds themselves, take the life force from the land and the trees, the mountains and water. We could do it, and we would under the End's orders.

A thought rose from the depths of our mind, one that harkened to memory—not mine, but the Angel's. We would not only do all of those things, we would enjoy them. We'd been created to kill. A thing that does what it was born to do was a thing that fulfilled its purpose, reveled in satisfaction, rejoiced with pleasure.

It might take some time to get there, but it would be inevitable. We knew that feeling deep in our marrow. I'd felt those things during my early days with the Order, when the mentors taught me my purpose in this world, the reason for the gift and curse of my magic.

I never thought I'd go back there, but I'd been fooling myself. In the face of horror, if a person couldn't fight, they'd retreat. Rationalize. Make might into right and black into white, evil into justice.

The path to that place from right here and now was clear as a summer morning. If the Angel and I fell all the way into darkness, we'd never again reach the light.

We sent a last message to Faith: *Find your own way back. Get out now. Get out—*

Our heart began to glow, not with the End's power, but with something unexpected. Something that didn't belong to us.

Magical flames flared within the muscle, burning away the strands of the End's web. The fire reached from the depths of our chest to lick our ribs—to strain forth from confines of our skin and spread across our chest. With the flames came an explosion of emotion. Of feelings that had no business rising.

In the place of despair, hope. In the place of hate, love. In the place of rage, a compassion so fierce, it took our breath away.

It tasted of grass and earth.

The heart link had died with us. It hadn't been reborn. It shouldn't be here. Red shouldn't be here, but he was. If he could fight for us, if he could keep the End on the ropes—

We grabbed hold of Faith's hands and yanked her close. We tried to speak, but our voice refused to obey. Thoughts would have to do.

Wrap your arms around our neck and your legs around our waist. Don't let go.

She didn't hesitate.

We gathered our strength into our legs and sent up a prayer to all the powers. The shortest path to our friends. No obstacles. Nothing in our way.

We leapt.

For a heartbeat, our wings wouldn't move. In that space, the hope and love and compassion threatened to desert us. We willed muscle and bone to their intended purpose, the reason for their creation. We filled them with our magic, trusting Red's to hold the End.

Our wings caught the smallest pocket of air, lifting us an inch off the snow. Then two, three. We sent all our strength into gaining altitude, foot by foot, yard by yard. With every stroke, the snow receded beneath us, gravity's grip loosening until it seemed to release us altogether.

We flew into the mouth of the tunnel through which we'd fallen, sliding from portal to portal, passing from one world to another. The stink of sulfur fell behind us. The burnt earth on all sides of us began to heal, the scent of clean, rich earth rising where before only death had reigned.

That couldn't be because of us. We were Death, not Life. But the sight and smell of it infiltrated our senses, strengthening us. The stroke of our wings grew more powerful, our passage easier.

The End hadn't set any snares on the way out. He hadn't expected us to leave except under his thrall. He'd counted on that.

We'd given him every reason to believe he couldn't lose. He'd laid trap after trap, and we'd fallen into every one of them. We hadn't even been able to avoid Dream's entanglement.

The End thought he knew us. He still did.

Red's magic kept him busy, but it didn't stop him from trying to find a way through to take over, to make us his, to take his due.

If we managed to uproot him out and throw him out, what guarantee did we have that we'd get all of his contagion? What if he left the smallest of seeds behind, needing only a touch of watering over time? What if everyone who'd ever been touched by him ended up like Mark, taken over and used up until no life remained, only to have his heart stopped somewhere far from home?

What if we were thinking about this all wrong? What if, over the millennia of the End's existence and his thousands of years of infecting humans with his emptiness, he'd touched not some of us but all of us? What if we'd encountered him early and often, and the idea that we'd ever been free of his nihilism was an illusion?

What if he'd gotten to me, Night, long before the Order?

Did it matter? We could wonder for the next thousand years and never know the answer. In the end, it wasn't important.

As a child, I'd been considered too dangerous to be allowed to live. The contract on my life had been placed by a Watcher, a follower of the Angel of Death. The Angel had been imprisoned by the Order, and so had I. The Order's ultimate mission had been the End's mission.

Too many intersecting paths. Too many for a coincidence.

Even if the Angel and I managed to pull the End out of our body, to send him away for weeks or months or years, he'd come back. He wanted us. He needed us.

He would never stop trying to find a way in to the source of our magic.

It hurt, the physical pain of the End inside of us worse than any pain we'd ever felt, growing deeper and wider and bloodier by the moment. His touch was vacant, devouring, desiring only death. Everything his fingertips brushed—his consciousness, his voice, his breath—turned to emptiness.

Having him inside, with Red's magic battling to keep us wholly ourselves, felt like a whirlwind. One moment, we were alive. The next, negated, nothing where our light should be, with only the shadow of our silhouette as evidence we'd ever existed.

There were lights at the end of the tunnel. City lights.

We rocketed through the last of the distance to the surface, bursting through into chaos and confusion. In the absence of the darkness the End had built, the lights of buildings and bridges and head- and taillights reflected on the surface of the Willamette, backlighting the army of spirits forming seemingly from nowhere at the water's edge and marching on Sunday and Miguel.

Famine had Beth backed into the base of the Hawthorne Bridge, the battle between them turned from physical to the soul-level. Famine caged Beth against the concrete with her arms, her head bent forward, her forehead resting on Beth's. We couldn't see Beth's face, but from the tension that wracked her body, she was losing the fight.

The Angel and I arced toward the brick sidewalk, feet connecting with earth, the impact sending us to one knee. Faith fought to be released before we could let her go. She tumbled from our embrace and rolled to her feet, taking in the situation and whirling toward Sunday and Miguel.

She ran for them, shoving them off balance and back—away from the line of spirits descending on them. Her hands sparked with the Awakened's light. The fire expanded, flowing along her edges, illuminating her every step with a blur of flame and iridescent light.

Her actions were so unexpected, Sunday and Miguel didn't catch themselves or push against her. It took them a full second to dig their feet in. In the space between, a line of familiar people materialized in front of them.

Red. Stacy. Ben. Corey. Jess. Addie. And twenty others—spirits, not living humans.

The spirit standing beside Addie held her hand. He was taller than she was by a handful of inches, his dark hair cut close, the black curls of his beard trimmed neat, his eyes the color of mahogany. He wore a sharp navy suit, the shine of his dark shoes melding with the grass underfoot.

Her husband.

And beside him, a line of his people and hers, ancestors going back generations, come to stand with her—with us—in this fight.

They were what she and Corey had cooked up, the something—someones—special. They'd come of their own free will. They belonged to no one except themselves, and they'd bet their souls on Addie. On all of us.

Addie turned to Sunday, but she'd already taken off, racing toward Famine and Beth. Addie kept moving until her gaze locked on Miguel.

"Help Night," she said. "Now."

He looked at the Angel and me then, eyes widening. He didn't see his friend. He saw only what we'd become—everything he didn't want to be, everything he wanted to run from. We read that in his face for a moment, and then the moment was gone.

What could he do for us? How could he help? He was a chameleon running borrowed magic, the power to smite strong in him. The righteous fire of an archangel flowed through him.

He threw back his head and shouted at the sky, the sound of his voice a beacon and a benediction.

"Michael!"

We gasped.

We'd envisioned that Michael would be needed. That he wouldn't pass up the chance to get in on the fight in the human world in a more visceral way. That he could be our wild card.

We hadn't counted on him.

Calling the archangel meant waiting for him to stand us up, to arrive after the fact, so late that his presence made no difference at all. It meant asking to be told what to do and how to do it, threatened and blackmailed, even if what he demanded spoke more of fear than hope, even if you knew in your bones that what he wanted was wrong.

The sky didn't flash with lightning. The air didn't bend and catch fire. Time did not stop.

But Miguel did. The fire of him grew wilder, stronger. His fiery halo became more than an overlay for his bruised-purple chameleon life force. It became multi-dimensional, existing in this world and every other. Looking into his eyes, we saw our friend recede and the archangel who'd demanded the door into him come to the fore.

He walked toward us, heedless of the battle joined behind him, of the Watchers as they pulled apart the threads that the End had sewn into the spirits of the dead, leaving bleeding souls in their wake. Of Red stanching the flood of life force from their wounds. Heedless of Sunday pulling Famine off of Beth, or Beth's collapse, her consciousness spiraling away. Of Faith on her knees beside Beth, frantically working her magic into the girl's body, trying to right a stuttering heart.

Michael closed the distance between us, coming to a halt inches away. He met our gaze, his fire to our ice. We saw what he wanted—what needed to be done. We would never agree to it if we had a choice. Every other time before, we'd had one, but this time we had only the choice to trust.

We nodded.

Michael curled his right hand—the hand that wielded the sword of protection, the sword of a god—into a fist. It roared toward our gut, striking with the force of a god, stealing our breath. His fist penetrated flesh and muscle and blood and bone, angling up toward the heart. His fingers moved within us, grazing organs and darkness, grasping and strangling the End's web. Yanking it from where it anchored, every last root and every last seed.

If the pain of carrying and fighting the End had been a horror, his removal was worse. The places the End's threads had embedded burned and ached as if they'd been frostbitten, some dead and gone, some regenerating. Our heart raced as we tried to contain the scream that clawed its way up our throat.

We tried to hold onto it, to swallow the poison in it, to keep it from ramming through our teeth into the cold night. We couldn't stop it. It refused to obey.

Out it came, shattering the air, cracking the glass of office buildings and windshields. It rent the darkness of the sky so deep and wide that for a split-second, the light of the stars and the sun shone through before the velvet dark flowed in again, coming home. The stars glowed brighter behind the curtain of night, calling our name.

Michael pulled it all from us—the agony and the emptiness—dragging it into the fire of his halo. The flame flared as it consumed this powerful piece of the End, extinguishing it from this world.

As the fire grew higher and hotter, we saw things in the deepest, hottest part of the flame that we'd never seen before. Righteousness, of course. A true cause for war, too. Those, we understood. Those, I, Night, expected.

But also fierce love. And strangest of all, hope.

The wound Michael had created in our body closed on its own, knitting, healing. The sound of his voice, at once too big for the world and soft and close enough for my ears alone, seemed to help.

"Darkness is not bad. It's not evil in and of itself. It's part of life. You know that better than any of us, don't you, Night? Or should I call you Death?"

Our words tumbled out like a prayer. "Night, please."

Michael's lips curved. "Darkness can turn, though, as can light, when they're used to hide the truth. When they turn, they need the opposite to remember who they are."

We understood—as Michael said, better than all of them. We understood secrets and lies. We knew what it meant to kill, what it meant to die—and what it meant to be reborn.

"The only way to air out what hides in the dark is to drag it into the light," we said.

He rubbed his palms together, as if washing them of the End, at least for now. "You know this isn't over?"

We nodded.

"You have the reprieve you need to grow into what you are now. Use the time wisely. Your family will want to help you. Let them."

We furrowed our brow. Would our family accept us? Would they still love us? Or would we find ourselves on the outside, looking in?

"Night," Michael said, "for once, will you do what I ask?"

We made him no promises. "Stacy needs that angel feather. A white angel feather."

"For what?" he asked.

"For once, will you do what I ask?"

He laughed. Just as suddenly as he'd taken over Miguel, he was gone, leaving our friend spent and on his knees on the cold brick, the night air around him singed and smoking, a single white feather clutched in one shaking hand.

We knelt beside him, but he waved us off.

He choked out a single word. "Beth."

We pushed to standing, stalking toward the fight near the base of the bridge where Sunday rolled on the grass in a deadlock with Famine, the Horseman thrusting her magic into Sunday as if stabbing her with knives.

Famine saw us coming, dislodging Sunday with a kick to the gut and rolling to her feet. Legs wide, hands drawn into fists at her hips, she challenged.

We lifted our left hand—not the hand of righteousness, but the hand of the heart—and closed it into a fist of our own. Ours didn't threaten. It didn't rail. It drew all the heat from Famine's body, swallowing it whole, leaving the Horseman shivering and devoid of the rage-fire that fueled her magic, leaving her with the only thing she had left: unrequited desire to be anything except the monster she'd become, and the jealousy that accompanied that desire.

That was what lay between her and Beth. Envy. And something more, something we never would've predicted, that Famine would never admit to, that Beth would never see and understand. A twisted kind of love.

We saw all of that in Famine, and she knew it. She hated us for it.

"Go," we said.

Famine didn't attempt to fight us. She had nothing left with which to fight.

We shot a single seed of her power into the air between us, watching and waiting as it opened into a portal, its hunger a match for Famine's.

The Horsewoman leapt through the doorway to powers only knew where. It didn't matter. She'd be gone a while, rebuilding what we'd taken. Plotting. Scheming. Growing her anger and envy and love. She'd be back. We'd be ready.

Faith's voice tore through the night. "Mom!"

We ran, dropping to our knees beside her, taking in what Famine had done to Beth—the wounds in her soul, the broken heart as it skidded to a stop in her chest.

"Is it too late?" Faith asked.

We shook our head. For Beth, it would never be too late. That was her fate. Immortality. Pain. And the thing that was sometimes hardest of all—living.

Her soul began to rise from her body, a ball of light the same color as her orange-and-black halo, winking like firefly on a summer's night. It gravitated toward us, landing within the cupped palm of our hand.

Faith sucked in a breath. "Is that—"

"Yes."

"What happens now?"

"We can place it back into her body, but we need your help. And Red's."

She turned to call him, but he was already running our way, the sound of his footfalls on the concrete loud in sudden silence.

He squatted on the other side of Beth's body, his gaze grazing ours and Faith's. The tattoo on his chest glowed white-hot.

"Heal her heart," we said. "Do it well and as quickly as you can."

We remembered everything she'd said about what it felt like the last time she died, her fear of going through that again, how long it'd taken her to get over it. Malek had put her back together then. He would know she'd died again. He'd know when we resurrected her.

We couldn't tell Red and Beth how to heal Beth, but we didn't need to. They carried the knowledge within. Pure magic. The Sacred Heart.

Moments later—moments that would feel to Beth like an eternity —we placed Beth's soul into the cradle of her beating heart. The fire of her magic flared. We let out a breath we hadn't realized we'd been holding.

And our phone buzzed. An incoming text from twenty-two-hundred miles east and south, from the heart of Snake Bite Tattoo.

We plucked it from our pocket and read.

I'm coming.

"Malek will be here soon," we said.

"And where will you be?" Red asked.

We looked at him, at the fear and hope in his eyes that he tried to veil. We heard the trembling in his voice. Felt the pull of the heart link between us. It was a miracle, that connection.

There was so much we wanted to say, so much we wanted to do. Instead, we stood and turned to look past Sunday, who gathered herself and rose from where Famine had thrown her, over to the battlefield where Corey, Ben, and Stacy stood beside Addie and the spirits of her loved ones.

The spirits the End had commanded had fallen, every single one. They needed deliverance. A path to rest and healing. They were ours to watch over, to care for, to help. Them, and one other—Mark. It was the least we could do, and we would see it done.

Michael had asked us to let our family do what they could for us. Right now, that meant taking care of each other. Cleaning up the magical mess we'd left here. Making sure any innocents caught in the crossfire had their memories wiped and a hot meal in their bellies. They would do all of that without question or complaint. Without us.

We had a job to do. "We have to take them."

"Take them where?" Faith asked.

"Wherever they want to go."

Red said nothing. His unspoken questions filled the space between us.

We glanced over our shoulder to meet his gaze. "You'll know where to find us."

The question was, would he try?

CHAPTER 18

THE ROOM FELT the same as it had all those years ago, like shelter from the storm. It smelled nothing like it had in Sunday's memory, or ours for that matter. Rather than shampoo and soap and sex and night terrors, we breathed in stillness, silence. No one had slept in the double bed since we'd left the Order. It was almost as if the mentors considered the space to be cursed or haunted.

Or both.

The bare mattress was dusty and lumpy, as were the tops of the pine nightstands on either side. The mirror over the dresser on the opposite wall showed our reflection, lit by the uncovered overhead bulb in the small closet beside it.

We looked exactly the same in so many ways. The shape of our body, the lines and curves of our face. The wings folded tightly against our back. But the star fire that ringed our pupils now stretched to a corona that obscured the whites of our eyes. The brown of our skin had deepened a shade. It felt cool to the touch, but not cold. The ice remained on the inside, a weapon to deploy when needed.

The sun had risen and set since we'd left our family to take care of and transport the souls of the dead. We'd come here as the moon climbed high, the balmy Texas weather a gift after the Portland snow.

The climate control operated intermittently, leaving the compound overheated inside, raising a film of sweat along our skin.

If we'd expected to find another soul in the Order complex in the middle of the piney woods, we'd been wrong. The operatives who survived our invasion and the mentor's demise had run, or been transferred or terminated. The only residents we'd come across were mice, cockroaches, and a raccoon.

The collection of pebbles Sunday kept by her side of the bed, brought home from the riverside where we'd passed our first survival test and been allowed to live, were still on top of her night table. We discovered the Our Lady of Guadalupe medallion stolen from the scene of my first kill on the opposite table. It was a wonder that Sunday hadn't thrown it away or destroyed it. I'd left her when I left the Order, after all.

We took it in hand like the charm against evil that it was. We sat on the bed with our knees drawn to our chest, back against the wall, and waited.

And waited. With every passing moment, our heart broke a little more.

From here on out, nothing would be the same. We'd been through changes before—huge, earth-shattering changes—but this was so much bigger. It felt final. We didn't want it to be.

Where did we go from here?

This was the last place that we had lived as a monster. Trapped in a cage in the bowels of the Order, in the no-man's land between the human world and the angelic realm. Trapped in an assassin's quarters, taking orders, killing and killing until the act of taking another's life led to soul death. Held captive to serve the Order's purpose.

We hadn't been human then—either of us. We weren't human now. We were something else, except for the heart link to Red, its fire burning brightly in our chest, its warmth a counterpoint to the chill. A reminder to remember who we were.

That was why we'd come back here. To remember who we'd been. To remember who we'd chosen to become.

We breathed in the scent of brine and the light of the moon before we sensed movement and a flash of blue from the corner of our eye. Anger welled in our heart and in the pit of our belly, our magic rising raw and wild inside, overflowing our skin.

Our visitor paused her step. "Are you going to try to kill me, *nena*?"

We wanted to lash out. To make our *abuelita* feel the pain she'd caused us. But the transformation already felt like too much to handle, our nervous system overloaded.

We exhaled a six-count, inhaled for four, and exhaled again. Slowly, our magic receded.

"I'm guessing that means no," Dream said.

We cleared our throat. "No. For now."

"I'll take the temporary reprieve," she said. "May I sit?"

We turned our head to take her in, our gaze sweeping her light blue shirt, sleeves rolled to the elbows, her denim pants, her bare feet. We looked her in the eye, expecting to see ambivalence at best, coldness at worst. Her face was filled with love.

The hurt and anger inside turned to confusion. "Why are you here?"

"To explain," she said.

As if anything she said could make up for what she'd done. "It's a little late for that."

"It's very late, but what we want sometimes takes a back seat to what we need."

We closed our eyes so tightly, we saw stars. "No riddles. Speak plainly or get out."

"You realize it's hard for me to talk in a straight line?"

Dreams didn't manifest in a linear fashion. They were made of images from our subconscious, our deepest, darkest fears and our highest, brightest hopes—the things we ran from, couldn't bear to believe, or couldn't bear to live without.

"That's too bad," we said.

She took a deep breath. She exhaled moonlight. We couldn't see it, but we felt its radiance on our skin.

"Look at me, *nena*."

We met her gaze.

"I love you," she said.

We refused to believe that lie. We refused to even hear it. "What you did to us—"

She finished my thought. Twisted it. "Had to be done. There was no other way to make sure that the worlds would have a chance to survive. Do you think I wanted to do that to you? That I wanted to break your heart? To harm you?"

We stared at her. "There's always another way."

She shook her head. "I have obligations to things greater than myself and my beloveds. When I come to a crossroads—when my only choices are to spare those I love or spare entire worlds, entire peoples —I must make the difficult decision, and I must make it every time. It's built into who I am, what I am, the role I play in the unfolding of time and space."

What did universal questions—and, if we believed her—universal decisions have to do with us? We'd needed her. She'd betrayed us. "That's not enough. You're not enough."

"I am what I am," she said.

That was something a god said. The thought hit us like a slap in the face.

Our *abuelita* was a god, not an ordinary grandmother. That she'd spent so much time with us, providing a troubled and sad child with shelter from the storm of her magic and the inevitable consequences to everyone we cared about—that part had been the aberration, the one thing she'd never been obligated to do.

She'd never been made responsible for loving us.

"You loved us anyway. You didn't have to, but you did."

"It was never about having to love you. You made it easy by being who you are. I may not be enough, *nena,* but you are."

We could barely breathe.

"The worlds need an Angel of Death who is committed in every way to the side of life. More than that, the worlds need an Angel of Death who understands what it means to be human, whose humanity is not only important to her, but remains the most important thing."

She laid a warm hand on our shoulder. "You said before that there is always another choice. Do you truly believe that?"

We nodded.

"You believe it because, for you, it's true. You always find a way, even when those of us who ought to know better can't see a different path, can't make a different choice. Michael, Gabriel, the other Elders—we have never been human and we never will be. You, my beautiful rose, understand what we never could and never will. *That* is why I did what I did."

It made sense. And it still hurt.

She'd talked about our humanity, that which we'd lost in the transformation—that which remained in our heart. For us, it had always and ever been about the heart.

In forcing us to become one, to become Death, she had made us what she was. An Elder. A being with obligations beyond those we owed to the people we loved. We might be called upon to make a decision like the one she'd made for us. No, not might—would. It would happen. It was inevitable.

"You begin to understand," she said. "It will take time. Hopefully, not too much. The path forward is still critical, and we need you."

We spoke with more confidence than we felt. "We'll be ready."

"I trust you," Dream said, as she had in the basement. She rose, taking her moonlight with her. "Can you forgive me?"

We wanted to, but there was too much to think about, too much to feel. We mirrored her words. "It will take time."

"Hopefully, not too much," she said again. "I love you, *nena*."

She faded as she had before, leaving a pool of salt water and the fleeting reflection of the moon behind—and the smallest bit of ease in our heart, along with the knowledge that we would see her again. We knew it in our deepest places, and we held fast to it.

Afterwards, we slept and woke and slept again, the images in our dreams and nightmares blooming in noir-stained grays. Flashes of color. Flashes of light. The spirits of the dead we'd ferried to their next destination. The hope we'd felt as we left them there—in the arms of loved ones. At the start of a new adventure.

The weight that settled on the bed beside us, that drew us close and spooned behind us, felt like a dream. Like the kind of wish that we had no right to ask for or expect. Like the kind of wish that would never again come true.

It smelled of grass and earth. Its strong arms folded around us. It whispered our name, breath warm on our skin. It spoke in Red's voice, east Texas drawl a balm.

"Are you real?" we asked.

Red didn't answer out loud, choosing to tighten his hold on me, to make sure we felt him. "Sunday's outside."

"The room or the compound?"

"The room," he said. "She won't come in and she won't stay here at all beyond sunrise. She said to tell you that so you don't get any ideas. You can't stay here. We won't let you."

We exhaled a shuddering breath. "Where will we go?"

"Home."

What did that word mean? For the longest time, it had meant Faith, and it still did. It meant the rest of our friends and family.

"Are they okay, the others?"

"They'll live, thanks to you."

"We didn't do anything," we said. "You saved us, all of you. We were so determined to do everything we could for you, but in the end you're the reason we made it through."

"You can't carry the weight of the world on your shoulders alone. You can't save everyone all the time. Sometimes, we save you. That's how it is. That's how it'll be when you come home."

He'd used that word twice now.

"You're wondering about me," Red said. "What happens between us."

Words felt treacherous. Nothing we could say would convey the depth of fear in our heart. How could we be scared, given what we'd become? What did Death fear?

Not life. Not forever.

Loneliness.

Could we stand on our own without him? The thought of it hurt so much, it overwhelmed. A wave of fear and grief crashed over us, threatening to pull us under.

Our heart had broken so many times before. It had healed every time—imperfect, but whole. We would find a way.

"Night?"

We nodded instead of speaking. It felt safer, even if safety was an illusion.

"I don't know," he said. "That's the truth, Night. I have no idea. I know what I want. I know what you wanted. But how things stand now? What's possible? That's something else. We're gonna have to figure that out."

We pulled away from him, allowing enough room to turn over, the mattress springs objecting. We needed to see his face. To look him in the eye, take in the lines etched at the corners of his eyes and mouth. "How can you be so—"

"What?"

"Calm? Steady? Strong? How can you not scream and rage? How can you not fall apart?"

He studied my face the way we studied his. "Is that what you want to do?"

We spoke through clenched teeth. "Yes. No."

"The alternative to calm and steady and strong is that I have to think about losing you. About whether I've already lost you. I can't do that. Do you understand?" He raised a hand to cup the side of our face. "Jesus. You're wondering whether I can still love you. How I can still love you."

We stared at him, unable to respond, afraid to move an inch.

His voice shook. "You think I give up that easy? Is that what you think of me?"

We'd hurt him. We'd made him doubt. Fear or no fear, we couldn't allow that to stand. "We're not the same. We'll never be the same."

"Neither am I, Night."

We blinked at him, our vision clearing enough to see beyond ourselves, beyond the stories we spun to take the place of the truth between us. We looked at him. Really *looked.*

His grass-and-earth halo had shifted, the colors deeper and darker, as if soaked in rage and tears. The lines on his face had multiplied. His skin looked too pale. He should be in bed back in Portland, resting and healing, not here with us.

The fight in the basement and at the waterfront had changed him in ways that had nothing to do with us. He'd seen things, done things, that he couldn't unsee or undo. His heart was raw, his own fear close to the surface, threatening to run wild.

Coming here for us cost him, but he'd done it anyway, willing to pay that price or any other.

A wise man told us not long ago that we carried the core of who we are into everything we did, everything we became.

We swallowed hard. The heart link flared.

That miracle was proof that, even if we had no way back to who we'd been before, we had a way forward. We had only to take the risk. To see it through. It was a jump from a high place, hoping to all the powers that Red would catch us.

We knew our own heart. If we refused to jump, we would never truly know his. We would never know the truth of what we had. That was the choice. It was always a choice.

We leapt, the shaky ground of fear falling away beneath us. "We'll go with you."

Red pressed his forehead to ours. "You want me?"

"We do." There was nothing we wanted more. "We love you."

His lips curved. "I'm gonna have to get used to that."

"What?"

"We." After a moment, he said, "Can we go now?"

We wanted to. But going meant questions and intense conversations and more change. It meant confusion and challenge, surrounded by our family. All of them. Right now, we needed Red, and only Red.

"Can we stay here?" we asked. "Just a little longer?"

He nodded. He planted a kiss on our mouth, tentative at first, then tender. It tasted of love and hope.

We would leave for Portland in the morning, but in that kiss we started down the path to the home that mattered most.

If you enjoyed this book, please consider leaving a review. It doesn't have to be long—even a few words will be very appreciated.

Reviews make it possible for an author to continue writing books in a series. They make a big difference in helping to get the word out about a book or a series. And reviews can make the all difference in the world when a reader wants to take a chance on a new author, but isn't sure whether they will like the book.

Thank you for taking hours out of your busy life to read. I hope this book brought you time to escape into a story, and that it brought you joy.

Turn the page to read Chapter 1 of
Angel Burns, Book 6 of the *Soul Forge* series.

ANGEL BURNS - CHAPTER 1

THE FULL MOON stared down from a spring sky awash in stars and wisps of cloud. A cool gust from the east lifted the long dark hair from our shoulders, caressing our skin like a lover. Its temperature, warmer than our chilled skin. Its perfume, tasting of pink and white cherry blossoms and the musk of the Willamette River that bisected Portland, cutting us off from our family.

Them, at Addie's house on the east side, snug in their beds and trapped in the smothering arms of their dreams. Us, on the west side, perched several stories above SW 5th Avenue, the downtown streets deserted below.

We were still unsure of each other. They wanted me to reassure them that enough of the Night Sanchez they'd known remained. To make them feel more comfortable with the fact that the woman they loved had become one with the Angel of Death. We wanted them to understand the ways in which we'd changed and what that meant, even if we didn't understand it all ourselves.

It was normal. Human. Something we no longer were.

We sighed, the movement undulating from lungs and heart to the crown of our very human head and down over the black wings folded along our back. It'd been three months. We'd done our best to understand and integrate our new normal. But we had obligations bigger than family, more important than love. How long before those responsibilities took us away?

A swift intake of breath and the deliberate crunch of gravel underfoot told us we weren't alone a heartbeat before the air filled with the scents that spoke of home. Grass and earth.

Red knelt beside us, salt-and-pepper hair floating with the breeze. The bright green and rich brown of his halo—the manifestation of his life force and flavor of his magic—deepened. He reached up to smooth his mustache, the barest touch of southeast Texas in his voice. "Here again?"

"We like it here."

"The view?" he asked.

The view was spectacular. Every line and curve of his face, the breadth of his chest beneath the unzipped heather-gray hoodie and black T-shirt, the muscular thighs inside his faded jeans. We wanted him here and now.

We always wanted him, but the strength of it, the insistent heat low in our belly, was new and seductive and slightly alarming in its lack of inhibition.

We swallowed hard. "It's the company."

Although we adored his, the company we referred to crouched across the street above the green tile entrance to the Portland Building—Portlandia, thirty-four feet of copper woman in classical clothes, trident in her left hand, right hand reaching down in benediction. To others, she was a statue. To us, she was a goddess frozen in space, the protector of the city. Her eyes gave nothing away. She seemed inert. But we knew better.

She was alive, like we were alive. We could smell her, all the copper reminding us of blood. The world didn't see her clearly. They saw what they'd been taught to see.

"She have anything new to say?" Red asked.

Our lips curved.

He poked us in the arm with an elbow. "She smiles."

"She understands us," we said. "Is everything all right? No

Horsemen of the Apocalypse on the stoop? No one tied up in the basement? No attacking hordes of possessed people?"

"None of those. Not even an archangel."

Archangels were trouble. We'd had to revise our opinions of them —of Michael, at least. He'd come through for us. We had to respect that, even if we couldn't count on it happening again.

Michael's absence should've felt reassuring. Instead, if felt like—

We met Red's green gaze. "It's the calm before the storm. The hush before the dawn."

"The moment before the other shoe drops. That's why you're really here."

To be alone with the protector of the city. To figure out who and what we'd become. To work our magic as it manifested for us now. To be ready to fight at full power when the battle came.

We nodded.

"Michael said we'd have some time—for you to get used to being Death, for the other side to figure out their next step. But I can feel it coming, whatever it is."

It could be the End again, the enemy who'd been there before the beginning of creation and who sought to destroy all the worlds, to return everything and everyone to the void. It could be the remnants of the Order of the Blood Moon, the magical assassins to whom we'd once belonged. Or the eldest Watchers or the Horseman Famine, or any of the others who'd come down on the End's side in this fight.

But we didn't think so.

"The fourth Horseman," we said.

"We can't stop that, can we?"

We hadn't been able to stop our own change or the transformation of our friend Luna into the Horseman Pestilence. Destiny seemed to want what it wanted, the rest of us be damned. "The odds aren't good."

He mulled that. "What do you want to do?"

"Look for her."

"You're assuming it'll be a woman."

"The rest of us are."

He inclined his head, giving me the point. "You getting on that right this minute?"

"At three-thirty in the morning, with no clue yet where to go?"

"So you're coming home?"

"That's why you came to find us?"

"Why else?"

He'd driven downtown, somehow managed to get into a locked building, and made his way to the roof to find us? Unlikely. "How did you get here?"

"Stacy sent me."

Our witch had teleported him. Previously, that kind of magic had been reserved for emergencies. For battle. Were we an emergency now?

Red furrowed his brow, reaching out to cup the side of our face. "I can see what you're thinking. Answer's no."

He could more than read our face. He could feel every emotion that coursed through us via the heart link we shared. For a moment, the sacred heart tattoo on his chest flared, the fabric of his shirt unable to conceal its glow.

Lines etched at the corners of his mouth seemed starker than they'd been a minute ago, as if the depth of feeling in his heart hurt him.

The last battle against the End and the living humans and spirits he'd hijacked had done Red considerable damage. He hadn't come clean about what had happened at the house after it had been invaded by the souls of the dead, their touch colder than the grave and just as fatal.

We'd seen only a small part of his fight. Spirits rising through the basement floor, busting through the protections and taking down Stacy—and with her, almost closing off the magical connections between us all that we'd used as a lifeline to help each other. To survive.

Red had saved her. We didn't know how. He'd refused to tell us, and the others who'd been with him kept mum as well.

At first, we'd thought he didn't want to burden us during our own time of healing, but as the days had passed and he'd avoided the subject, we understood that he was hiding it. Maybe hiding from it. We didn't know how to help him, except to give him time.

We raised a hand to cover his, to press his palm to our skin. "What do you need?"

"You." He leaned over to brush his lips across ours.

We caught his bottom lip with our teeth as he pulled away, drawing him in, deepening the kiss. We fisted a hand in the fabric of his shirt.

He laughed, his breath warm and inviting.

"Home is overpopulated," we said.

"I'll grant you that, but none of the houseguests are sleeping in our room."

We glanced away, our eyes drawn again to Portlandia. She hadn't moved an inch, her copper body frozen by the hands of the sculptor who'd crafted her. Maybe it was our imagination that muscles moved beneath the metal, that a voice issued forth from her still mouth. That she called our name.

We rose on steady legs, an inhuman silhouette in the dark, all dressed in black. Our wings unfurled to full width.

Red whistled. "You're something, you know that?"

We did. "We can fly you home."

He shook his head. "No need. Stacy gave me a return ticket. You can be my passenger. Where's your backpack?"

The backpack meant to conceal our wings. "We didn't bring it."

"Night, you're gonna get yourself caught. Seen."

"By who? The Portland Police Bureau is out in the streets looking for angels?"

"Bullets might not kill you, but they'll fuck you up," he said. "Sort of like what'll happen if the normals on the ground catch a glimpse of a woman with white fire in her eyes and giant wings. This is Portland, and people don't bat an eye, but when you take off flying, they're gonna figure out you're not wearing a costume."

He was right. We knew better. But we also wanted to feel free.

The Angel part of us didn't care much about human concerns, but the human part of us put them first. It was stupid to give in to the desire for complete freedom. If there was anything we'd learned over the years, that kind of freedom was as much an illusion as safety.

We folded our wings down to their most compact, a foot's worth of feather and muscle and cartilage. "Better?"

"Grab onto me," he said, rising to his feet. "Don't let go."

We wrapped our arms around his waist and held his gaze as the night began to spin. Moon and stars and streaks of cloud and copper goddess. Concrete and glass and steel. A single houseless human, all his worldly belongings in a green trash bag, settling down for the night on the sidewalk beneath us.

The air exploded in sulfur and heat. The sensation of being violently yanked through space pulled us across the city, the lights of the freeways and their reflection on the river a blur of light.

A heartbeat later, our feet settled on the front porch of Addie's buttercream yellow house in the glow of the overhead light, boards creaking underfoot. The big tuxedo tomcat who called the wide porch rail home had gone hunting for the night. Or fled from the predator in the rocker beside the door.

He smelled of ancient paper and millennia, his silence so thick, it took on a life of its own. He had no halo—not a halo full of emptiness, like the End, but no halo at all. He pushed to his feet, his white shirt bright in the dark. The black leather duster he wore skimmed his black leather pants, billowing around the soles of his motorcycle boots. He wore power as if he'd always had it, as if he didn't need to prove himself to anyone else.

That was true freedom—the power to make your own choices, to own them, to live with them.

If the consequences of what Malek had done from his creation as the serpent in the Garden of Eden through this moment tore him up inside, he didn't show it. If he wanted to scream to all the heavens and all the hells with the pain of it, he never would. The End had taken away his voice, the voice of temptation, forever.

Forever was Malek's reality. Now, it was ours, too.

Fear took root in our heart for the first moment since the time just after our transformation. We slowed our breathing, drawing out our exhalation to a six-count, inhaling for four, calming our nervous system so we could focus.

The serpent hadn't planted himself in that rocking chair to meditate or ruminate. He'd been waiting for us.

Malek raised his hands and signed.

We need to talk.

ABOUT THE AUTHOR

Since the age of seven, Leslie Claire Walker has wanted to be Princess Leia—wise and brave and never afraid of a fight, no matter the odds.

Leslie hails from the concrete and steel canyons and lush bayous of southeast Texas—a long way from Alderaan. Now, she lives in the rain-drenched Pacific Northwest with a cast of spectacular characters, including cats, harps, fantastic pieces of art that may or may not be doorways to other realms, and too many fantasy novels to count.

She is the author of *The Faery Chronicles* and *Soul Forge* series, two complete series of urban fantasy novels, novellas, and stories filled with found family, angels, assassins, faeries, and demons.

Connect with Leslie
leslieclairewalker.com
leslie@leslieclairewalker.com

ALSO BY LESLIE CLAIRE WALKER

THE AWAKENED MAGIC SAGA

THE SOUL FORGE

(The Complete Series)

Angel Hunts

Angel Rises

Angel Falls

Angel Strikes

Angel Roars

Angel Burns

THE FAERY CHRONICLES

(The Complete Series)

Faery Novice

Faery Prophet

Faery Sovereign

SHORT STORY COLLECTIONS

Ink & Blood

Ink & Stars

Ink & Sword